ALOCASIA

alocasia

*99 queer writers
on plants and nature*

Sarah Clark & Ashely Adams, *editors*

ISBN 979-8-218-85582-6
Library of Congress Control Number on file.

Cover and interior design by Alban Fischer.
Printed in the United States.

Supported by funding from Accelerate Resilience L.A.,
a sponsored project of Rockefeller Philanthropy Advisors.

ARLA

https://alocasia.org

To those who garden fearlessly.

Contents

Introduction

Nature is a queer thing and plants may be the sovereigns of Nature's Gay Agenda. I say this not with the cheeky academic's wink and nudge but as an observable, practical truth.

Plants happily try on all manner of sexual reproductive diversities and even perversities. Flowering plants favor androgyny, growing both male and female reproductive organs within the same bloom (funny enough, this is botanically known as a "perfect flower"). They weave ecosystem-wide polycules or sometimes shrug their metaphorical shoulders and reproduce asexually, reconstituting themselves from branch or pup or bulb. I don't even want to get into whatever the bryophytes are up to.

We humans are not absent from the queer lifestyle. Purposefully or not, we evangelize these deviant botanical wiles to every corner of the world–tickling stamens and dampening nodes. These are acts of survival, curiosity, and affection.

The writers collected in this anthology explore the ways in which we build community with our queer non-animal relatives. Quite literally, in "Plantcestors," Rebecca Kinkade-Black puts forth "'We are all connected' / is not just some trite phrase." Furthered by Anangookwe Wolf who mournfully declares in "i want clean water goddamnit"—"i don't want concrete / i want clean water" for us and for our plant relatives. Our planty genealogies give way to so many models of relationship from the meditations of Ena Elder-Gomes' "My father carries a jungle" to a strained relationship with a father in Ann Tweedy's "inner limits"—"my love for you could be / a potted orchid: chipped bark, / climate control, delicate / watering preferences." And the remembrance of a nurturing mother, in Saida Agostini's "I write of my mother in the book of joy"—"even in winter she is pledged to nursing life / in the bitterest of Maryland snow, think on the four lime trees / sheltering in our house, by the dining table."

Sometimes, things don't work out as we hoped, as Keagan Wheat writes in "Our Breakup Plant"—"You picked a name / without a square of sunlight / for a fucking succulent." Sometimes we face what's toxic, and our own toxicity, as Maya Cheav explores in "the masochist and her lamprey" — "I live on your mattress, caked with dirt and dog hair, / confronted by the stain on your pillowcase saying, / 'this is your mess too.'"

Sometimes, we're as deadly as what's hurt us — "In a few weeks, the message is clear and green: his face above the words 'Abusive Scum.' Pictures of my creation start appearing online, from people I know and from strangers," Raina K. Puels imagines (we'll give them that plausible deniability) in "Moss crushes in my closed fist."

Or, we become heroes, like Ellie Howard in "Seedbombing a Golf Course" — "I glide across the sidelong path each day, / considering the best-suited plants / to seed along the fairway / succulents for the sand, / shallow-rooted crops for the putting greens." Plausible deniability, again. We challenge societal wrongs, ever becoming societal norms, as Nora Hikari docs so flawlessly in "Exposition on Pears, as a Transmisogynist" — "What shape is a pear? What is 'pear-shaped?' / What audacity, named after itself."

Plants guide us through challenging the social expectations about our lives — "While you're horizontal on canvas furniture that / doesn't look the way it did in the catalog, slick can in hand / cold condensation, you're supposed to say *this is the / life* when really you should be asking *is this my life*," writes Rita Mookerjee in "Cardboard Cutout Palm Tree." Or, as Chiara Di Lello interrogates in "Childless Millennial Considers Non-Attachment" — "*I don't want* is a cardboard box kissing the curb / full of what could not bring me use or delight / while new breathing space moves like a child / through my finite sunlit rooms."

Through the imagery of agriculture, through the very ideas of who we nurture and let grow, these poems ask important questions about who belongs and who has been shut out of natural spaces. "Underneath the fields is where our stories are buried. The monocrops were decisions made about our past, so I ask you to take the batteries out of the clanging wall clock before I go to sleep to prevent the supremacist art of domestication from permeating my dreams," writes Nikki Wallschlaeger. Or as Aerik Francis writes in, "An Anti-Pastoral" — "In this pasture I assume a posture / as if confronted by hungering animals. / I am praying they see me as merely docile."

Through nature, we reconsider the tolls of capitalism and corporate landscapes — "because HR says: studies show / the presence of plants is soothing / to clients and hey, I like them too," begins Esmé Kaplan-Kinsey in their must-read "the office/the after." While Umang Kalra, musing on mushrooms (forgive us, they're not truly Plantae) writes, "At the end of the next apocalypse when all the people are gone, will / the internet try to kill everything else," in "REMEMBER WHEN THEY TOLD US THE MUSHROOMS COULD TALK." Margaret Saigh takes it a step further — "On a podcast I am told to imagine / all the roads in all the cities / filled with plants and trees and paths for people to walk," in "THIS IS AN AUTOMATIC REPLY."

Queer sensuality is something we're far from short on, as Miriam Navarro Prieto explores in "Borago Officinalis as Pleasure" — "climbing / up my calves: unexpected scent of chlorophyll, the warmest / flash of indigo coming up my thighs." And the tortuous yearning in March Abuyuan-Llanes' "Dry Love" — "its countless seeds like / arrowheads pricking the skin / of my calves and / thighs while I / turn restlessly in my / sleep."

Maybe it's fitting that it was the beginning of the pandemic that reconnected so many of us with nature, and that saw the birth of this magazine, that now, as we look ahead into an uncertain future, especially for those of us who are queer, or love those who are queer, we take into account Tristan Richards' words from "Pandemic Plants and Disco Balls:" "Maybe all I need to do is notice that the snake plant / is still standing. Maybe today, it's okay to rest / on a simple fact and pick up the dropped leaves later."

In editing this anthology, we tried to assemble a broad taxonomy of voices, species, cultivations, sorrows and joys. However, scientists and artists both know the work is never done. There are always discoveries to be made and we have only just begun to spread our shoots.

Touch grass,
Ashely & Sarah

"i love it when people, plants, and poems are gay"

—CHEN CHEN

Rasha Abdulhadi

Romancing the Artichoke

oh darling it's been so long
and you've been made so
tender by time, succulent at the root,
past prickle and thorn
as I peel each leather leaf
of your protective petals
butter you up, my lips and teeth
seeking succulence at the root
peeling toughness tenderly,
taking my time with your trans-
luminescence by candlelight
considering every fold, every
layer's transit, take you to me
with the soft music on
letting fiber be fiber, accepting
only the cleft ridge of sweetness
watching your colors change by candle flame
a sunrise disrobing your pinks,
your creams, your dusks relishing
the almost entirely edible middle of you
and at your sunflower heart, the delicate choke
of finest slivers of sharpness
silvered hairs precisely held aside, and you,
thorny again at the center,
a tight clutch over your seeded trove
softly softly, I know not to tongue
the spines or take them too personally

or give up, no no, not me, as I press my
nose against floret, three fingers upon a pedicel
denude of petals, the pretty-tough tasty-sharp,
and open wide to take you whole.

March Abuyuan-Llanes

Dry love

I.
In Laguna, you wake me up at dawn
to pick wildflowers with you
on the coconut meadow. As we walk,
tumbling from flower patch to
flower patch and stems between
our fingers, I tell you what each
is called: the magenta ones,
malatungaw; the little violets on
wicks, *kandikandilaan*; and
the pale butterflies with
the fragrance of ginger and
sampaguitas, *kamia*.

Later, in bed, you ask me
what these are, the itchy
grass sticking out of
the hems of our shirts and
all over our shorts. *Amor seco*,
I say, meaning, "dry love"
in Spanish. Seeds which latch onto
any passing hair and
thread of yours with the hope of
finding themselves elsewhere with
you, eventually.

Tomorrow, will you
remember all
these names I've told you?

II.
Back in the city, you
are gone and so are the flowers
we picked together. But the amor
seco remains, on my clothes and on
my blankets, wash after
wash, its countless seeds like
arrowheads pricking the skin
of my calves and
thighs while I
turn restlessly in my
sleep.

Ashely Adams

Prescribed Burn

Wildland Fire Use: *The management of naturally ignited wildland fires to accomplish specific prestated resource management objectives in predefined geographic areas outlined in Fire Management Plans.*

There is a scrub preserve south of Tampa Bay where the grass kisses at your legs with ungentle tongues, growing up golden-brown between the tooth-edged saw palms. Compared to the concrete buildings and exotic trees, the scrubland feels exposed. The naked sky's brushed by scattered groves of pine, the trees all maintaining a polite distance from each other. Time it right and you can watch the slow drift of the sky into the magentas of sunset along with the silhouettes of whippoorwills sweeping overhead.

Despite the relative proximity to the city, almost nobody uses the trail. It's one of the few places I have been able to find in the city that gives me any sense of isolation. No traffic, no emails, no roommates forgetting to take out the trash.

No man tailgating me, laying into the horn because my bumper stickers displeased him.

No man refusing my help on a paper because he doesn't think I know what climate change is.

No man screaming bitch at me for the crime of not looking at him while we pass on the street.

Yes, only me and the armadillos crashing through the undergrowth, unafraid in their pursuit of all the rewards of the soil.

Test Fire: *A small fire ignited within the planned burn unit to determine the characteristic of the prescribed fire, such as fire behavior, detection performance and control measures.*

Before I moved to Florida, I worked at the Hiawatha Visitor Center, nestled against Lake Superior in Michigan. Most of the guests were families, scout groups, or white boys in their early 20s slightly smelling of weed. Occasionally, though, a woman came all by herself, picking up maps and putting them back while waiting for me to finish helping a tourist find the boat tour. I knew what she wanted before she approached me; it's rare someone chose me over the older men that worked with me.

The woman leaned over the counter. "Do you hike around here often?"

Of course.

She inclined her head, whispered conspiratorially, "Is it safe?"

I smiled. Told her there was nothing to fear but bug bites and sweat and mud. Safer than the city. A party. A college dorm. The greatest threat is always another person, not nature.

But the woman already knew that, didn't she?

Brush Fire: *A fire burning in vegetation that is predominantly shrubs, brush and scrub growth.*

I return to the scrubland again and again. Each time reveals a small new thing—a pond born from a midday downpour and the dragonflies that hover around it, tiny wildflowers dimpling the ground in purples and whites, the terns and gulls specking the sky on their way to nearby retention ponds.

Then, on one visit, I find swaths of the preserve burned, the sand crusted black with soot. Around the last few feet of the tree trunks, scorch marks stained the bark. I pause every few feet, snapping pictures of the landscape, careful of the tread marks left by a bulldozer. Someone else had been here and the place had burned for it.

Prescribed Fire: *Any fire ignited by management actions under certain, predetermined conditions to meet specific objectives related to hazardous fuels or habitat improvement. A written, approved prescribed fire plan must exist, and NEPA requirements must be met, prior to ignition.*

Some ecosystems depend on upheaval to survive. To replicate this, wildlife managers purposefully set sections of the land on fire to replicate these natural disturbances. In college, I once worked on one of these prescribed burns, one member of an unkempt gaggle of undergrad volunteers invited to a local Audubon sanctuary. The crew was excited to have us, handing out portable water packs and face masks. The burn boss, a man with some single-syllable name like Jeff or Mike, was less impressed. He looked each of us over, checking how capable we seemed, how flammable we were.

The burn boss stopped on me and my thick, shoulder-length hair, "Can't you put that up?"

I shook my head. Ponytails always gave me a headache. I didn't even own a hair-tie and the small percentage of our team that were girls didn't have a spare. The burn boss sighed, motioned to the sweatshirt I was wearing. "I guess if you pull up your hood that will be fine."

Pulling up my hood, I wondered if the cheap fabric was truly safer than my own hair, but I was happy to do whatever so long as I could stay. All I cared about was staying on this burn, seeing what a field looked like when it was on fire, nursing its heat and flames to its end.

Fuel Reduction: *Manipulation, including combustion, or removal of fuels to reduce the likelihood of ignition and/or to lessen potential damage and resistance to control.*

Here is how you stay safe: don't start a burn when the humidity is low; don't burn on a windy day; wear your hair up; don't wear your hair up or someone will grab it; wear a mask; don't go out at dark; don't be by yourself; hold your keys between your fingers; come up with a plan of attack before arriving at a burn; at a bus stop; in a parking lot; consider the ecosystem requirements; check the weather before leaving.

Underburn: *A fire that consumes surface fuels but not trees or shrubs.*

The only time I have ever gotten mad about being catcalled was when I was birdwatching along the Dead River in Marquette, an hour's drive away from my visitor center job. It was late fall, the ground hard and bare from cold, as if preparing itself for the blanket of snowfall. As I was observing the geese and ducks huddled along the shoreline, a man driving past yelled something about my breasts, which were buried under a winter hunting jacket. He sped away too fast for me to talk back. To ask him if he knew how hard it was to adjust binoculars with wind-nipped fingers or to identify a rare gull out of a flock of thousands? All the time and effort to become a good observer lost in a second to a honk and shout. Why not wait until I was walking to a class or to the mediocre sandwich shop?

Didn't he know what landscape he belonged to?

Structure Fire: *Fire originating in and burning any part or all of any building, shelter, or other structure.*

On the day Christine Blasey Ford testified of the sexual assault she experienced by Brett Kavanaugh, I went hiking at the scrubland. The ground was still scarred from the burn but saplings were already hiding the worst damage under the soft shade of their needles. Palm and yellow-rumped warblers chirped from the bushes, trying to lure my focus to their bounce and cheer. And, God, I just want to watch them and think of nothing else but the way they twitched their tails, but I couldn't stop thinking of the hearing. Couldn't let go of the spectacle of it all—a woman forced to recount the worst day of her life, pull it up from the sludge of trauma to be dissected by old white men who couldn't imagine what hurt felt like. How they would prod for any fault in a narrative that's edges were softened by decades, not because they cared for the truth, but because they wanted to get all this mess done.

It wasn't just Ford I thought of either. I thought of all the people, distant and close to me, who watched the shadow of their own assaults in the hearing. A friend, a family member, an actress, an online acquittance, a coworker, another friend.

I'd hoped the openness of the scrubland could soothe me, but the sand and the heat only made my body ache. Still, I plunged on down the path. Better to let the anger crackle in this underbrush than to sit and wait for the end, the smirk and whine of a man who wouldn't face any consequence. Better to walk through mosquitos and the ugly return of pine hammocks to the land than wait for the inevitable end where nothing changes at all.

Escape Route: *A preplanned and understood route firefighters take to move to a safety zone or other low-risk area, such as an already burned area, previously constructed safety area, a meadow that won't burn, natural rocky area that is large enough to take refuge without being burned. When escape routes deviate from a defined physical path, they should be clearly marked (flagged).*

Because of my hair, I was the last one of the prescribed burn volunteers to get equipment. The boys had snapped up the pile of bladder bags, perhaps imagining themselves as heroic firemen maneuvering the fire with arcs of life-saving water. All that was left for me was something that looked like a garden tool made by demons to poke sinners in hell. At the end of a cumbersome wooden handle was a wedge of metal split with a hoe's edge on one side and thick tines on another. The burn boss nodded and told me the tool was called a McLeod. I couldn't imagine what use I would be to the effort besides raking up after the smoldering remains of the men, busy work retribution for my styling faults.

Our fire crew wandered across the grassy field, dipping their driptorches down into the grass. The dying foliage of autumn lit up under the stream of gasoline. Some of the other volunteers gasped as the fire sprang up to heights over our heads, the air filled with the scent of dozens of bonfires. The burn boss tapped my elbow and gestured towards the arc of fire pushing out and out towards the trampled perimeter of where the burn should stop, "Do you see that grass on fire? I need you to break up the clumps."

I wanted to say back that of course I could see the fire and what did he want me to do about it with the McLeod until I saw what he meant. In between the strongest points of the inferno were clumps of grass inelegantly burning. I didn't understand why those charred lumps mattered, but I was eager to redeem myself from my earlier hair mistake. I hopped through the gaps in the flames and brought the heavy McLeod down, smearing the cinders into the dirt until the grass became flat ash against the Earth. I hopped from hot spot to hot spot, smashing apart the vegetation until my arms strained from hefting the McLeod and the smoke fell thick over the field, hiding everyone else from view. Looking back, I should have been scared. For all I knew, the fire could have surrounded me, cut me off from escape. Yet here was peace, me and the job in this burning world.

Initial Attack: *The actions taken by the first resources to arrive at a wildfire to protect lives and property, and prevent further extension of the fire.*

When I worked at the visitor center, men would ask me if hiking was safe in the forest as well. They would call me up and ask, "Can I bring my gun with me?"

Wildland Urban Interface: *The line, area or zone where structures and other human development meet or intermingle with undeveloped wildland or vegetative fuels.*

People don't understand why we would want to burn the land, to stop the field from its growth into a forest. They fret about the boys clipped down from the men they might become, molded by feminine hands into something soft and willowy. Isn't it dangerous to start a fire? Isn't it possible we're accusing an innocent man of a crime.

And here is how I would answer these questions. I would tell them that that stagnant woods is no home for the scrub jay, the grasshopper sparrow. The pines will die with no offspring to replace them in the shade of an old, dying bough.

Come, let us watch this hillside burn, its smoke pleasant as it stings our lungs, its gray and crimson smell lingering on our clothes months after, as if pleated into the fabric. Press it to your nose to remind yourself what a healthy destruction smells like.

Fire Storm: *Violent convection caused by a large continuous area of intense fire. Often characterized by destructively violent surface indrafts, near and beyond the perimeter, and sometimes by tornado-like whirls.*

Here is the part where I am supposed to tell you why I am writing this. Tell you about the time a man hurt me that made me feel this way. The time a man followed me around the city for stopping to look at gulls. The man who screamed at me about how he couldn't have his gun. The man who tried to steal me away at 14 during a concert to "dance". The man who stood too close to, grinning as I looked at swimsuits in a Wal-Mart.

The truth is, I've been lucky it's just been that. Maybe, instead, I'm supposed to tell you the story of those who haven't had my luck. I know more than enough stories to give the needed climax.

That's what we call the last stage of succession of a forest—the climax— where all the trees are old, giant, and all stagnates in their shadow.

This is what I'll tell you. Someone took a photo of me at the prescribed burn. In the picture, there is nothing but smoke and me, my body obscured by a neon safety vest. My face is equally hidden, by hood and face mask, the only thing visible is a lock of hair and the glint of my glasses. I've had some people say I look very scary.

So, let's imagine all those abusers stumbling through the burn site, smoke so thick you can only see the faint curve of hills. Let's imagine the fire distant, but still a threatening aurora on the horizon. Let's imagine a figure emerging, framed by the wilting stalks of grass, body cloaked by gray and protective cloth- ing. Let's imagine the dreadful thump-thump of something heavy and metal hitting the ground, coming closer.

Let's imagine that they will know a woman's fear, even if it's just for a moment.

Mop-up: *To make a fire safe or reduce residual smoke after the fire has been controlled by extinguishing or removing burning material along or near the control line, felling snags, or moving logs so they won't roll downhill.*

The obvious signs of fire have disappeared from the scrubland when I hike there. The plants have reclaimed every bare inch. The dirt is smooth after months of Florida storms, the imprints of truck tires and boots gone. But if you get down close to the Earth, you can find a small plant with spindly stems. Coated with silver wooly hairs, the plant looks cold, frosted, even in the Florida heat. On the top is a rosette of yellow flowers the size of a thumb.

This is the Florida golden aster, a rare plant that is endemic in the Tampa Bay area. It grows nowhere else in the world. For decades the population had been in decline due to habitat destruction. Scrubland, viewed as useless and ugly, was destroyed to build up housing developments, condos, and shopping centers. Without this scrubland, the Florida golden aster clung to life on the margins of land development, a being that could do no more than survive under beings more powerful than it.

But, sometimes, we listen to what nature tells us, usually when she gets sick of our shit and sinks our homes into a limestone grave. Now, there are preserves like this one I hike in where we promise to do better. To protect and nurture the most vulnerable. It's not close enough; life can only flourish so far in isolated pockets of safety.

Still, I bend down, watch the shiny-winged insects cling to the aster's petals, and think a better future is possible. One where we listen to those who have suffered. One where we let the fires burn.

Saida Agostini

I write of my mother in the book of joy

most evenings find mummy pacing down cooling
paths in a blaze of blossoms. nothing that lived in
guyana can be nursed here, so instead her resistance
is found in the bud of hydrangeas, gladiolas, and a love
of hummingbirds. the most common of flowers
will be tended — during the summer she glories in the
rightness of blooming, dedicating hours to pulling
errant weeds that choke the root.

 even in winter she is pledged to nursing life
in the bitterest of Maryland snow, think on the four lime trees
 sheltering in our house, by the dining table, forcing
my blustering father to cower at least for a short while
in its branches, neighbors come by to exclaim
at the impossible orchard reared among wood planked walls.

my mummy the stubborn farmer, laughing proudly
by its fruit. requests for advice returned with exacting
directions on wind, sun, and timing, yet when my sister
and I hear her, what we think of are two little girls
reared less gently then this — her a young lonely mother
 with sometimes brutal hands, but here I am
crying at the lesson of her bowed back in the garden,
hands dug into a mire of dirt, stubbornly
willing love into life.

Ashia Ajani

After

"And when the earth defends you, you become its lover."
—*Here and Elsewhere* (1976)

Sun-spilled. Filled with so much song, even the cicadas paused their chirping to hear the melody of a new world overflow. These songs were how we kept our memories alive, embarrassing as some may have been. Nobody wanted to recall the seed patents, the plastics littering poorly maintained roads, how an extra dollar could afford you another day's survival. The babies, brown and plentiful, couldn't remember a time when the earth wasn't their playground, when the sky burned crimson, when the saguros collapsed from exhaustion. They thought our generation strange: the way we still flinched at the sound of thunder, reminiscent of the bombs and shrapnel launched in the name of progress. How we sometimes ate until our bellies hurt, or searched for our car keys, now obsolete. Occasionally, an elder would pass a body of water and weep, the memory of drought so deeply embedded in their soul. Sometimes, hope is more painful than enduring: but now that we've survived, we live our lives at a ship's helm of our own beginning.

And in the After, folks would tell us this interruption was as short as a hare's tail, when it really came down to brass tacks. A minor tear in time's good dress. A terrible dream unraveled by weavers in search of the cross stitch. The storytellers wanted to rewrite the whole endeavor as a trickster's parable, but the ones who survived held their memories in dog-eared pages. Collapsed, oil-slicked. Grandmother undid her braid and soaked up all that grease, clipping the ends as a testament to what we were leaving behind. Sent the prayer floating down the river, a funeral pyre. We only cut our hair when we are in mourning. So the morning came, illuminated. We watched how beautiful a thing could become when it is returned to origin—again cell, again egg, again portal. Again, lover, palms berry-stained, grasping the future with both hands.

Eventually, America became an afterthought, easily mistaken for the rush of wind that picked up pollen and carried it to other lands. We became other lands, buoyed by our ancestor's insurgence—how they greened, cracked, crumbled whatever asphalt tried to silence their transformation. Our *gritos* & gumbo ya yas filling the night sky instead of exhaust. They knew, without a doubt, that even when habitats crumble, some brave creature comes to nest in the ashes.

We met at the crossroads, throwing seeds instead of salt. Let us bloom here, a green insurrection. At the edge of a new world, a figure waits at the mouth of the moon, hips rocking like boats on brackish water. Saddling dusk, she dreams of semi-aquatic guppies inching towards the bowl's inverted rim.

Mair Allen

In Spike, In Bloom

The edges of the orchids' frilled petals ripple.
Thrilled. It lives a little. Until.

Did you ever kill an orchid? Of course I did.

Did you love it? Obviously. Oh — The killing?
Or the thing itself?

Would it be wrong to say yes to everything?
I filled the window with plants and my love

said it was too much, but it was me

who let them dry up. I didn't know
how to care for so many at once, they all

under saturated and me, over committed.
Have your plants ever gotten gnats?

No, I love them with benign neglect.

And the yellow flowers tremble at that.
Not you though. Feel how

absorbent the moss,
how rich the thick chipped bark. This all

will hold your vellum roots. I will
love you different. Here, a bottle of mist.

Here, a silver bowl of spring water
for soaking on Sundays.

I have never loved anything

like I love your tender petals. I will learn
to care on time, in time, for you.

Ally Ang

Invocation

Let the moon wobble.

Let the basil plant flower.

Let the poets discombobulate.

Let the verbs noun.

Let the nouns verb.

Let the grief howl.

Let the emails unread.

Let the land speak.

Let the oceans revenge.

Let the people free.

Let the people free.

Crisosto Apache

from *Swift Cinder*

for Milton Apache

buckshot splitting air, cracking space, ricochets off tree bark, tree limbs

scattering brush   climbing

high up into Bear Canyon, into the mouth of the sky

—Wednesday, April 09, 2014, roughly around 3:00 in the afternoon

a specific moment and time

no different than the odious Big Bang

setting a single course of action   as a determinant event

billions of years in the making

first refractive light against planets and stars

lifting split light   against lit faces

bringing a specific moment   fastidiously forward

toward a series of momentary collisions

Season Of Reformation (11/23/1990)

The Aspen's Turn: yellow, gold, and then orange

They fall to their final destination,

with one breath from their creator.

A slight rustle of a stream; in the cool undergrowth,

Where the deer take their last drink; before migrating

into the mountains.

The fresh snow falls.

A glimpse of an assorted array of confetti

A path leading up to the road; dead shrubs, and trees.

A few birds chirping in the distance

The sight of death.

The sound of life.

A dew-drop on a marigold

A touch of god.

A flower in a meadow

What makes you pick this certain one out

of a million?

envelopment of toiling flame   engulfing in combustion

gas, subatomic particles   obit out of control

nucleus circles   expansion girds into guard rails
     flying fenders

in swift swirls   of oil sludge, petroleum, plastic, and
metal

—the gestalt sending his ghost into nearby thickets

—in a dream

he devours kisses (11/23/1990)
as night follows daybreak,
spring calls the rain-washed valleys
and a butterfly passes through the rows,
apple trees turn a plum purple
to a flourishing flush with white edges
furnishing the garden

leaves susurrate, drowning his plea,
they feast on another butterfly,
which lands on the apple tree branch,
sharp slivers sink into the butterfly's
head and thorax,
tree limbs devour the butterfly
as apple carcasses litter the grass
he is still afraid

a circular wave intertwines his hands,
first right, then left, reminding him of butterflies,
weaving his fingers into the tree branches,
what remains is the pungent smell
of wilting pink blossoms
as he tries to escape, the cactus needles cling harder,
he screams as he reaches for his mother
laying beneath the apple tree

across the stream, a spider web recovers,
the butterfly had its leg caught,
but through struggle the butterfly recoils,
and becomes restrained,
—his mother faces upward toward him,
    but the stare means nothing
trees shutter in the distance, under the moon,
between two ridges, indigo skyline brushes against
the mountains, the apple trees lose their brilliance,
and flowers lose their prism,
spectrum rays cease to a cold grey,
absorbing our breath, our kisses

t'eesh [ash] flakes fall softly

t'eesh [ash] flakes fall in soft particles

t'eesh [ash] releases soft particles

t'eesh [ash] releases all particles

leaving a gold vacuum of space

[there]—kú'yuu

                                        kú'yuu—[there]

                [there]—kú'yuu

                                          kú'yuu and [there]

indiscriminate object strewn   forming dashboard
a quick buck shot echoing along,
                                Highway 70
the collision translates a probability   cohesion of metallic abrasion
                                        of beauty

upon impact   birds scatter, then cease,
and a resounding shotgun blast
ricochets off tree bark darting up the canyon
                                —over
                                —and over
                                —and over
                                —and over

an abbreviated oblique asymptote   never meeting its
                        predetermination
                        coordination
                        or terminus

Robin Arble

Sunlight in Late Spring

I am standing alone in an abandoned pasture, watching a tuft of marigolds burst through a tractor's ribcage. A huddle of brown cows graze in the shade of the forest's edge. Once they were sure no-one was looking, the marigolds pummeled through absolute blackness with the clenched fists of their buds, exploding into golden fire as they gasped for sunlight. Now the cows swat flies with their tails, the marigolds nod and doze in a cloud's passing shadow. Soon the cows will turn their heads and wander to watch the fully-bloomed marigolds lean a little in the bright breeze. Soon the cows and their calves, the marigolds and me—mothers, daughters, close and distant cousins, nieces, and aunts—will gather to stand in the sunlight no-one can touch. I know I will be the only creature staring across that sunlight who will see the abyss in our distances. But for now, standing in the shadow of this cloud, we are each an open secret.

sterling-elizabeth arcadia

transdesert gender tryst /
at the foot of mount wrightson

for aria / for evita

my baby
face a cactus
one too far to touch
a succulent
sunset portrait

at 5 o'clock come out
from your tile
your tucson stucco
take the sonoran
desert tread with care
about the sharp
thistled shadows
inhuman suns
play on organpipe stems

the greasewood
most sweet for you
smells of rain

velvet mesquite most touching
in its yielding pods
you find fruits you can consume

you and I both
know these
things before the saguaro

you seek the small the
soft and petaled

Guérin Asante

On the Other Side of Moss

*"Simple £1.25 natural cleaner removes moss
from driveways without using harsh chemicals."*

And what becomes of rain returning to crevices.
What feeds them to the amplitude of later days and suns.
How much nitrogen must then be bought to keep an oak from dying.
What, then, might be said about the names we lay about them.
Which syllables collide with them; which ones caress their green (or gray or orange).
Whether they can hear us.
How we think about what stones have been assigned to do to spite them.
If they tire of comparisons. Being addressed as lichen.
If they think they form a wall between convenience and future.
Whether they feel the world grow warmer in their shallow of their leaves.
And if this is like the last time, or the last, or the last . . .

lae astra

Callus

There was callus tissue on our monstera propagation
near the bottom of the cutting. I thought it was mold
and cleaned some off when changing the water.

I looked it up after and learned that callus are cells
that cover a plant wound. That the tissue has the potential
to develop into parts that the plant needs, like shoots

and roots, an attempt to focus its energy toward growth.
I felt bad for removing it in my ignorance. Apologized
to this monstera who has been through so much,

whom we first met at the plants floor of the Tokyu Hands
department store in Shibuya, "just looking" turning into
bringing the monstera home, the leaves facing outward

with us as the blue Tokyo dusk and skyscraper lights
melted into night. Our first plant together. You said
your dream was to live surrounded by plants overlooking

the city. A first step toward that, sharing breath
in the living room with our paintings and instruments.
The monstera kept going, despite mealybug attacks,

sunburn, rotting roots. One leaf after another
withered and dried. Despite the trauma,
the leaves we saved continued fighting to survive.

Energy from sunlight transformed into an expanding
network from callus cells. Primary, secondary, tertiary.
A few months after I first notice them,

enough roots have grown for our monstera to live in soil.
A shiny new leaf has just emerged. I can't stop checking it
every day. How incredible that they keep trying despite

so much loss. That from the wounds, they still bravely
send out bridges connecting them to life.

Bryce Baron-Sips

Grasses have joints when the cops aren't around: A sestina for the end of the world

Come, stand between a blowout
Breeze and tearable tallgrass that is joint-
Ed because of a student rhyme, that sedge-
S have edges and rushes are round, but
Grasses blow smoke in diploidal faces
Hybridizing as purer theories rust.

You see this fungus, this rust?
Ready as an engine is to blow out
An airplane of schaudenfreuding faces.
Shaved down features rattle, wealthy joints
These pearls they clutch between sweating fists, but
There are no prairie oysters in this sedge.

There is more to grass than sedge-
Lessness, more to time, air, and hosts than rust.
Puccinia graminis is all but
Wheat and barberry in endless blowout.
As crops get used to feeling out of joint,
We put on our more medieval faces.

Earth does prefer young faces,
But somehow, it's still kept its grass and sedge.
They evolve to the rhythm of a joint-

Relationship, reproduction and rust,
An airdrop arms race to nix a blowout,
A compromise with the wind again, but-

We can't right the craft with a rifle butt,
Even as the torpedoed plane faces
That there is no breakthrough SpaceX blowout.
There will be hybrid grasses, starlet sedge.
Whatever cannot out-drought or out-rust
Will see if it's meant to bend at the joint.

Grasses kiss wind at their joints,
The breeze and the leaf node nod in sync. But
Still the ragged pollen comes, still comes rust,
Still comes the shock of forgetting faces
Of pilots who can't tell what's grass and what's sedge,
Thinking fire, like candles, can just blow out.

Like a parent who faces a blowout,
We say Future went to live in the sedge.
We joint our lives, but it's to bend to rust.

June Beck

A text message to a New York Navajo

The ancestors are always with you,
even when you're smoking weed
in Central Park.

Greet them with every sunrise;
wear a piece of turquoise
in all your outfits.

And you will be blessed and loved
every day. Because every time
you do, they'll see you

And be happy.

Elizabeth Hart Bergstrom

For the Chronically Ill

Maybe you were meant to be a maguey,
an agave that takes thirty years to bloom in desert grasslands.
Your heart is intoxicating,
your sweetness distilled into mezcal.

Maybe you were meant to be a traveler's palm tree
on the island of Madagascar
that waits to be pollinated by ruffed lemurs.
Your nectar slakes the animals' thirst
and their muzzles shine with gold pollen.

Maybe you were meant to be a corpse flower,
lying dormant for ten years
and smelling awful when you finally wake,
but still, crowds of people come from miles away
to marvel at you.
You unfurl a ruffled spathe in the colors of
blood clot, black mission fig, deep purple bruise.
You radiate your own heat.

Seeking out the wind, water, and sun you need,
you will grow in your own way.
You don't need anyone's permission
to sleep for a decade
and only blossom for one day.

There are only the movements of celestial and earthly bodies —
there are no clocks that matter.

Jacob J Billingsley

case moth moth case

THE FELLED

our bodies plaqued with wet leaves in the seam of fall
shoulder out of enclosures stamped into the ground
as passed from hand to hand chipped nuggets of root go
with muscled vine and tendrils of fine resin dripping
on the smooth-of-dark sleep-cut stone in dim October
and this building calm in the slumping tug of the hush
our bodies plaqued with wet leaves in this seam of fall
move buoyantly in the twig-steam and spiced vapor
of the all-living duff as we assemble unknowingly
the mudstuck bower where we'll at last lay down

shouldered enclosure
bodies of   trees
masses of bodies
passed by censors
in-delicate embrace
sung wet outlines
are shown through
on the stacked wood
white drip of viscid
snug moonlight in rows
scented masses
the boys singing
passed by censers
in cords of wood
box-cities of it
the cricket captured
still giving, giving
invertebrate skyscrapers
to the duff
serving still
all   living
rain bringing
no censers
no smoke
just considering
cooling days
over endless chirping
we are
                    here
the scent of fire

[*LITANY*]

the burnt aspens
the eaten spruce
denuded
the hidden redwood
newborns chasing flames
a tree new to science
but known by its people
throughout centuries
of colonization
a specimen
may it go on
as it will outstanding
the worldwide gingko
famously forever
before Sycamore Gap
(felled)
after afforesting windbreak
(in-built)
a "great green wall"
to negotiate the Gobi
all who still hold up
streambanks against wash
who still hold down
sliding plates of soil
and fold the rocks
we carve our names in
the bark to burn off
even still then together
as mountains moving
three mourning cypress
in a German painting
and the ashes they cut
the ashes they cut

the Joshua poached
because we forget
how a yucca needs
the sand its moths
make habitat of
as we seem to need
anonymous lumber
chipped and pressed
the ply martyrdom
the bananas in rows
their pickers looked over
(faint scent fading by
old name of "Cavendish")
still freshly nursed
the two I forgot
but can see through this
a gift from the city
through this window
implanted street trees
where the city ashes cut
to hold back green
bejeweled invaders
these two need water
so in dry weeks I—
my hose a breast
my breath their air
my mulch a swaddle
the puddle of milk
on the sunken sidewalk
for my tulip and elm
my rosid and poplar
in loose yellow slump
leaf dropping summer
my lament dehiscence
but in this drought

yes I will too drip
and decohere
placefully made
a home for another

1. The shaking wind like the gush of breath I let out as a kind of sigh-huffed punctuation when the conversation sputters into the wet mud of my complaint like a refurbished Packard.

2. The unallocated desire that had burned in me for ten months already when the days went cool on us again.

3. The garden looking abandoned simply because no human had passed there and it was thickening with the wool of blown seed not far from its birthing grounds of next year just below where loose assorted wonderful vermin had turned the soil just by being there into a kind of dry mush that if someone did come along they'd find as pleasant to step on as one of those polyfoam mats you can buy at a bougie enough office store.

4. The tear in the fabric of text hampering the ergonomics of the passenger seat's pleather.

5. The way the winds drive harder in the fall because the jet stream still somehow comes down to our latitude following the seasonal descent of the sun.

6. Turbulent flow as an ongoing area of research.

7. More leaves falling when more wind is blowing.

8. The unallocated desire that has burned in me for ten years already.

9. Novel form as a passage to the end of such desire; the fact that no such invention should be necessary. That if I could speak plainly. That I do not see where we're going from here. Struggling to be okay with that. That I need more and I do not understand how this is not plain to you or how you could deny it to me. Every time you think I don't know what I need.

10. "Plain" being a long stretch of uncultivated field but homophonous with a kind of shaving device used to make things square and proper, or, in

circumstances demanding decoration, to add a straight line of curved ornament to a wooden surface.

11. Time-worn symbols of fertility complicated by the fact that we are both men still managing to manifest themselves as if they were unalterable truths.

12. The theory of metaphor as the structure of thought.

13. Literary inheritance as a valid but still deficient substitute for the continual creation of kinship. Having heard the words the Fisher King before I understood who or what it was. Knowing that was passed to me by a professor to whom it was passed by a long line of mainly men down from Eliot from all the way back to Chrétien des Troyes back on to the oral origins of the legend back on to perhaps another man whose inability to reproduce was more physical. My ongoing engagement with A. and other young poets by the acts of speaking, reading, writing, and thinking as an endlessly reticular or I should say rhizomatic continuation of such a line, "rhizomatic" being taken not so much from French theorists as from my own more immediate inductor whose name was David and whom I claim here as a forebear. This is all for you.

14. The industrial reversal of the man/nature divide as manifested in the fact that a plain is not an uncultivated field. A field is a cultivated plain.

15. The violence of feudal times and the mysterious wound of the Fisher King contrasted with the bureaucratic stranglehold of the adoption process.

16. The fact that I'm externalizing this to such a degree that I cannot admit adoption would be perfectly achievable but that it just isn't something you think we're ready for. And I know you're right, so instead I blame the state.

17. The recognition that if we were not both men it could happen just by accident. Knowing the terror of such an accident without denying what it would mean to me. Knowing that such a terror will never be mine.

18. All the times I've daydreamed of it happening by the accident of some family connection of yours needing a home for newly bereaved children. That

I can only envision such a scenario when it is paired with any given variety of societal collapse.

19. Knowing that wouldn't sway you either. Thinking I could even know that. Recognizing that in discussing the issue with you my expectation that you will always refuse its possibility (even when you explicitly do not) is itself a barrier to achieving its realization.

20. The salience of this issue, having derailed completely what could have been a perfectly plain, juicy, ominous narrative depiction of a common couple's argument that nonetheless would speak to some fundamental, fated disagreement, the plain truth being sometimes quite ugly, even technical when the mind is technical. Such textual ugliness an obviousness so naked that the performed circumvention of emotional pain gives the reader a direct but voluntary conduit for said pain.

21. This text still causing to arise in the writer an idea of the redemptive power of literature-as-kinship (repeat item 13). The unallocated desire that has burned through ages.

22. Whereas, having also just polished off the final changes of a poem for a dear junior writer who learns from me I can return now to a more proper allocation (dislocation) of said desire and write a beautiful poem. Something my body not only allows but would seem to require.

23. The dry mush of my bereavement. Its fictive nature its real nature. Its real nature one day coming about only by means of fictive elements. Washed by words and placenta. Made new because the soil when living makes itself new. All conditioned things bitter except for the spotlessness of bitterness well spotted. So I give it up. I give it all up for you. Repeat item 3.

24. Just by being there. Pain so naked it can only be yours if you choose to bear it.

Yasmine Bolden

cottagecore death fantasy

after janna ibrahim

what if, i propose to you after we whisper about my dying, *breast implants
could pocket all the plant stuff needed to become a tree? like, maybe
when i die, you scoff at a coffin knowing nothing can contain my
overgrown-ness and return me directly to the brown earthen hands
that know how to handle me better than this tupperware-obsessed world
ever could? like what is everyone always trying so hard to save
in those tiny tubs? leftovers? compost, baby.* it is a few sleepy breaths past
two in the morning and i can see the question in the curve of your neck
as you beckon me over. come here, *bring the meaning closer,* you say
without sound. i am always so afraid to touch you. not because of anything
you'll do, but because of the anytime of my die. you can laugh,
that was worded funny. on purpose, i pot my fluttering asclepias tuberosa
thoughts in vases too large and ornamental to do their job properly.
you stare at me, not intensely, and i'm reminded of how good you are
with a hammer. *do you want implants?* you ask, splintering my abstractions
with your bare fingers. *okay, stop, stop. what i mean is, i want to be a mother.
i know stems in stem who could make that happen.* your eyes
are closed now, tired and so softly alive. *you will be,* you say, as if
you don't know my body. as if our earlier conversation isn't rotting between us
as we speak, silently giving itself to the silly little green shoots of the fantasy
i'm trying to flesh out for us. can't you just let some part of me live a little?

Joefel Bolo

Kamias

For me, I understand why this is poignant. Grimace instead of genial—shape is different—genre so immanent. As a kid, this is the closest friend of a bitter melon. As if my forehead tells. Lightest of its small form, branches are old and spreading. Ode to sour flavor dishes. Because *Nanay's sinigang* is perfect—through this alternative mixes, effective in a natural essence. And extract the juice if you feel inclined—this *remember*. Leaves are downward, pointing low, and constrict your sadness persistently. I squashed its body and pitches my eyes. Blurred for a millisecond—to evinced joy. And the season of this tree, pops and germinate—*looking plentiful.*

Moss crushes in my closed fist

Moss crushes in my closed fist. I drop it into the blender with buttermilk. The whirr scares the cat, green eyes wide. She flattens into the floor, protecting her organs from the sound she worries will bruise or cut or maim. The noise ends. Everything is more quiet after a ruckus.

Wet electric pulp sits in the basin. I pour it into a bucket, check again that the door is locked, and wait until dark.

For weeks, I've hunted for the right wall. Brick. Centrally located, but not too public. Close enough to his apartment, but not so close he could see me on a midnight run to 7/11 for those jalapeño chips he loves. Even when his knuckles were bloody, he'd still shove his fist into the bag. He always complained of the sting, but I think he liked it: small pain as a humbling force.

Black pants, black sneakers, and black jacket clad I say goodbye to the cat with a scratch on her head. At night, our city is alive with college kids, drinking and laughing. To them, I'm invisible. So are the bucket and paintbrush in my hand. Especially now that the skin around my eyes has healed.

I walk to my large swath of wall. Between a coffee shop and a real estate office, I begin to paint. I've sketched this enough times. Proportions memorized. No one stops to ask what I'm doing. The slurry sinks into the brick, but dries light. Almost invisible. I stop by each night to water my work, spray it down. Moist. Vibrant.

In a few weeks, the message is clear and green: his face above the words "Abusive Scum." Pictures of my creation start appearing online, from people I know and from strangers. The cat purrs on my lap as the posts roll in. Some defend him. Others cheer on the vigilante artist.

A video of him goes viral. He's red in the face, huffing, clawing off the moss with his bare hands until his fingers bleed. After that, there's no longer any chance he'll come for me. The spores have already done their job, deep in his lungs.

His body won't be found for a few days. And when it is, it will look more like an emerald knoll than a human.

Moss is soft and resilient. Moss has a way of consuming.

Caroliena Cabada

Wild Onion

This morning is my favorite morning so far:
an east wind rustling through wild onion blossoms
just coming up, pale purple and thin. I wake
up from another

morning after, warm light—warm skin. Everything
west-facing: witness the end of another
era, another life, another inside
whispering to me:

I don't smell sweet, but I flavor this soft green.
Every dish lately is savory—I want
sweet melody echoes, a karaoke
tongue: sing another's

final praise song for a lover, bittersweet
tasting with all of your mouth. This morning is
my favorite morning so far: a little
taste of tomorrow.

Jody Chan

naturalization

—after Zaina Alsous

there was haddock baked in a metal tray
& a buffet of tiny square desserts, there was a view
of peaks, there were canyons & icefields & paths
descending steeply into graveyards, there were plastic
bags pledged to the wind & a black bear staring down
an orange flare, behind the verb & verb bars, the organic
olive oil boutiques, there were two humans
making their way slowly across the southward
rock face, sometimes kissing, there were park passes
to pay for & British flags splayed open on
the breeze, across from which the verdant slopes
boasted several golf courses, monocultured
for their insipid greens, there was the quiet drift
of continents, there were endangered minnows, algae
garlands in the sulphur ponds & tropical fish
released by aquarium enthusiasts, a faint lilt
of mist yielding to an orchestra of weathers, throughout
the designated conservation areas, the occupied
hands of labourers, numerous as mosses
& prone to erosion, there was moss, there were firs
& emboldened marmots, beyond the trail markers,
the gravel lots, at dinner an oil executive remarking
on his surroundings, sucking the meat off
a slab of bones & four floors below, a fawn
mere hours old, staggering into the woods

Maya Cheav

the masochist and her lamprey

the air is ripe with mildew,
its potent flavor percolates my lungs.
you overturn your leftover pizza
to discover black mold.
empty amazon packaging sits in the corner of your room
filled with soy sauce and ketchup packets
from a week's worth of door dash orders.
full bottles of medication
that your therapist insists you take
crowd your desk,
along with empty THC cartridges
and a pile of grubby styrofoam plates.
every other thursday
you come back from your film class,
storming in with a passion, saying,
"we should move to seattle!"
but it takes you one afternoon to remember that
you're failing school and
you got fired last week and
your car registration is expired and
we're two months late on rent.
I go to sleep to the sound of your voice
shouting while you play video games
with your friends until four in the morning.
I live on your mattress, caked with dirt and dog hair,
confronted by the stain on your pillowcase saying,
"this is your mess too."
your misery mixes with mine,

like a blood transfusion gone wrong,
and for a period of time
I forget that I am not your mother,
that love and torture don't have to exist within the same breath.

I dream of a house I can call my own.
there's a pot of plant cuttings by the windowsill,
the propagations brimming in sunlight.
the greenery stands tall
against the warm birchwood bookcases.
beside the salt lamp and the log stool,
a set of braided chairs sit perched beneath
the giant monstera in the center of the living room.
I walk my dog in the neighborhood
and learn the wheel in weekly pottery classes.
I make my pasta al dente with dried tomatoes.
I wear the color yellow.
but when dawn turns to dusk,
I turn out the big light,
and when I pry my eyes open,
I only wake to you.

Grant Chemidlin

Cruising

Two men meet in the middle
of a secret,

hide behind
the bushes. The trees,

who see no deviance, offer
their trunks for cover.

Two men meet in the middle
of desire, slip out

of their armor, bask
in the unclad sun,

in each other's arms,
in each other's tongues.

In the middle
of a better world:

Two men, undone.
Two men, unbelievably soft

when they touch. Even
the stubble-studded chins

are silken moss.
A twig-crack. A gruff shout

in the distance
& two men

disappear.
All that's left—two hollowed logs

holding their breath

on the forest floor.

Chloe Chou

supermarket succulent

perfect, and what does that mean? pink pot,
moist dirt, green leaves; factory made. how do you
produce a living thing? when you're something so
beautiful under supermarket lights, when you're
"CLEARANCE: $5 ONLY." when you're on the
cashier conveyor belt and then

downstairs in the living room, extending towards the
sun. stretching, distorting, finally imperfect, finally
alive.

Night Blooming Cereus /
Queen of the Night

(for Selenicereus grandiflorus)

We only ever had an apartment balcony, what my mother turned
into a small flourishing garden of pots spilling over
with what I didn't care to know about as a child.

After her third work shift, I remember her out there at night
bent over against the harsh moth-circled light, tending to quiet green
bodies that reached for her, as she stared out past the rows of cheap housing,
searching inside for her village horizon rice farm mother brothers sisters
back home in the Philippines.

I remember she would wake us up, bleary-eyed children,
and usher us out onto the humid apartment balcony
to show us the night-blooming cereus,
the wild bright opening,
a temporary queen bursting with fragrance,
a silent star stretched out heavy on a long pink neck.
        Look   she would say   *it only blooms once—*
fleeting beauty she served us with the weighted gravity
of losing thick in night's air.

We didn't care much for plants then,
for the display of green she quietly tended
after her third work shift, with her lonely heart.
Children don't care much for the toil, the ache,

the solitude of worry she must've desperately poured
into tender growing things,

changing it all into growth,
transmuting it all into night blooming,
into a balcony of flowering, into waking us up
in the middle of sleep without language to explain a love like this—

how she tended to us
two tender flowering things,
the toil   the light   the soil

between her tired
beautiful hands.

Seth Copeland

Caddo Creek

We've come past the creek, two boys and
    the indifferent lonely-
        ness of beasts.

You move to incept the hunt, redhead
    centipede scuttling
        over stones,

ready to chew me unfamiliar.
    We setae soften &
        morph, eyes locked.

Dusts us pollinate, we primrose moths
    topping wild onion blooms
        in the clear,

flecked till flesh was flower, unflowered,
    air wilted to dark crisp
        softly sewn.

We suck the cups, the bulbs, our sepals
    into windy glistens
        sweeping at,

whipping into each other's bodies,
    into a new body,
        one fleabane

fasciation freaking in dust gust,
     warping together in a
          cristate stretch.

Chiara Di Lello

Childless Millennial Considers Non-Attachment

And I am washed up again on the shore that is the green armchair
by its side table arrayed with my convalescent plants

          What, you too?

The ones who got too little, too much, or at the wrong time
stunted little alocasia who bent full over to burst one new leaf
from her one living stem

          Exhausting, this whole business of renewal

and the banana palm I nearly killed trying to kill its plague of mites
as cures go I'm worse than the disease

          Death to what? What's the motto?

I don't want. I don't want. Not being a Buddhist
this always sounded like recalcitrance.

          Now dear, don't be difficult.

I thought I was one of the hard to kill ones, good with whatever
until I nearly whatevered a pothos to death too

I don't want. I couldn't hear the freedom beyond that final *T*
barring strangers from a room of my own
the period's full stop turning the window sign to CLOSED

I don't want is a cardboard box kissing the curb
full of what could not bring me use or delight
while new breathing space moves like a child
through my finite sunlit rooms.

Sara Eddy

Plant Ethnography

In the corn museum the docent shrugs
when I praise the strange blue cobs.

They weren't good producers.
They were content to remain plants.

What did we give up when we abandoned
variants that were happy this way?

When the cactus evolved thorns,
retracting its leaves into daggers,

where did the sound of the wind go?
Does the cactus remember that flutter?

An artist and a scientist worked together
to record the cellular sound of the cactus,

its song in seed, genetics, body.
The sound is like poetry scraped over desert rocks.

When making a difficult decision,
imagine one part of yourself continuing

down the path you did not choose,
living her own life of hardship and joy.

Knowing she's there may make your decision easier.
Go ahead, imagine another life of blue corn & cactus leaf.

Ena Elder-Gomes

My father carries a jungle

At night I dream in green:
wet leaves pressed to my skin,
the hum of insects,
a jaguar's steady gaze
in the cathedral of trees above.

I have never felt the weight of Amazon heat
settle on my shoulders like breath —
but I've heard it
in the hush of my father's voice
when he speaks of home.

My father carries a jungle in his chest.
And when he breathes,
I can hear the vines moving.

He came from the belly of the world,
where children fall asleep in hammocks
beneath the open mouth of grandfather sky.

The stars blink like elders.
Marci Amma, moon keeper of stories,
cradles dreams
in her quiet light.

In the mornings,
the boys pick plantains for grandmother,
who fries them in coconut oil over flame —

sweet smoke curling into songs
only the ancestors remember now.

I carry it too, *La Selva*—
its language tucked beneath my tongue,
its rhythms stitched into my skin.

I do not speak
all my people's words,
but I hold the silence in my hands
as if it were a seed.

One day, I will plant it
in soil that knows me.

One day, I will open my mouth,
and a river will come out—
singing everything
I thought was lost.

Emdash AKA Emily Lu Gao (高璐璐)

Honeysuckles at Ocean Air Elementary School

Lonicera subspicata

San Diego sweet, dewgong[1] white honeysuckles fill the black vinyl fences, separating us kids from "the real world." As a daily ritual, I spend recess foraging them, plucking

honeysuckles off the fences diamond-shaped openings—today it's after I scrape my knit knees, the popular wasp kids don't wanna include loud me and my friends don't

wanna play more make-believe. I feel like the playground's tired rubber floor. At least there's honeysuckles: free gregarious snacks with petals flared like Farrah Fawcett hair.

Oh to bloom like you, graceful without the need for external praise. Ivory honeysuckles wear their emerald leaves like ostrich boas, happily surrendering to sprung play-doh

fingers who pluck your long stamen: coveted yellow straws springing out from the center. I suck on these for a butterscotch buzz. Can't recall who taught me to pinch them between my thumb & index: someone's older woodchip sibling? I shift my weight

crestfallen there's nobody to ask but roly polys and sage scrub. The honeysuckle haven turns my monkey bar hands sticky, the same hands that made oobleck & turkeys earlier.

Honeysuckles taste like caramelized fishing line, like how it felt to find 25¢ in my pocket for the gumball crank at Ranch 99, where I'll accompany Mama hangry

[1] Yes, the pokémon.

after Chinese school, like realizing I'm actually *early* to the function, not late, like
having punctual working parents ensuring you're not last at drop-off. One brother left

you for Middle School, the other for UC Irvine. I pull a wedding dress honeysuckle,
their rhubarb vines patient. They don't mind if I skip church or what I wear to church.

Honeysuckles are treats I sneak into DEAR[2] time (for girls I don't realize are crushes).
If I were one, I'd befriend the bumblebees I once feared but ache to be. Then I'd offer

extra nectar to good apples who dreaded going home like I did. Home: an empty two-
story conch shell, chaparral cinched, wonder what is wrong with me.

No honeysuckle reverie. Lonely in this unhappy-should-be-happy. I flip a tawny red
pillow to hide cheese puff fingerprints.   Laoye is a comma asleep on the sofa,

mandrake body snores, Chinese soap opera playing. How fun to leave this human skin,
be a honeysuckle with perfect pitch, naturally sweet integrity, turn drab fences pretty.

My stunning short life devoted to tasty feelgood, laughing ladybugs, mingling coyote
mint. My desire to be wanted won't be satiated by others: *I need to want myself.*

I need to want myself. Be my own bounty. Stop believing all I do is hurt people I love.

Learn from the honeysuckle halcyons of my past—practice memorizing my worth. I

need what feels feels impossible: an overdue rainfall of desire for myself, a rushing

deluge lining every curb   a majesty for myself   fig tree roots upheaving sidewalks.

[2] Drop Everything and Read

Danielle Shandlin Emerson

For the common sunflowers along the Upper Fruitland, NM ditch

How do I write
      a poem about resilience—
I want to talk more about the water,
      about streams and lakes.
Sun rays that never sit still.
      I imagine turquoise clusters,
matched with bright magenta masaní scarves
      tied around our wrists, clasped
cloth in our mouths. Wait / ałtsé'—watch, as wild flora
      and pollen twine along our skin
like wild horse hairs.

      How do I write a poem about resilience—
how many times will I be asked to write a poem,
      a song, a prayer, a sermon,
a land acknowledgment, an obituary—
      about resilience?

Instead, I want to talk about the slender riverbanks,
      the farmland ditches that masaní told shí dóó shícuzzins
not to jump in, because 'waterdogs,' imaginary beasts,
      might drag us under.
I want to talk about childhood dirt banks
      covered in wild sunflowers.

Taller than my seventh-grade self, arcing like the rez cats that
        come and go, always coming and going.

Shimá used to drive us down the ol' back roads,
        I'd slouch in my seat and stick my feet
out of the window—squealing like a toddler
        every time a sunflower touched my toes.

In the rearview mirror,
        I watched their sturdy stems spring back up—
arching as if they held the sun.
        How many times will I be asked to write a poem
about resilience?
The wind spreads their seeds, their roots become
        clenched veins, tethering.
I want to walk more in beauty, in memories
        and blossoms that kiss my skin.
And I wondered if that dream counts as
        resilience.

Cherolyn Kay Fischer

ode/*ode'*

I.

with your medicine
we can talk with plants
in their own language
gleaming green resounding
in eardrums, throat, and heart
we sing to roots and chlorophyll

II.

open us wide like a spiderweb
stretching to all corners of the world
alive, enchanted, trembling
like shadow and snow
songbird and butterfly
mossy rock and stormy sea

III.

dance and remember

Aerik Francis

An Anti-Pastoral

It's not the right word—wilderness.
Living in this dream I find little sleep.
Instead I find myself taken

by the sight of shitting sheep
that cough & simultaneously excrete
blackish-brown blueberries
& piss a sour amber puddle.

Here I am simultaneously
medicinal & poisonous—
I make a move & artificial

light obscures the touch
of starlight. Where is the Sun

whose rays feed the greenery,
heat the humidity, but whose
face turns away from me,

whose countenance, when
encountered, was neither
yellow nor red but white?

I want to say I admire the birdsongs
but they deny me rest. Ducklings that flinch
at my gestures to quench their thirst.

I feed & pet a dog, neglect the bark.
A spider swings until smashed
between a pillow & my head.

Mosquitos halo me in the umbra
of branches & leaves hanging overhead.
I wax bucolic to the trees & my buccal void
fills with insects. I am bitten & so I retreat.

I'm afraid of everything here: the concept
of property, the potential claims of trespassing
by the neighboring settlers. Three white boys,

shirtless, approach on bikes & interrupt,
asking if I live here, where the owner is,
if I know ash, if any of us are cops.

Crops. In this pasture I assume a posture
as if confronted by hungering animals.
I am praying they see me as merely docile.

How pathetic. Every day roosters escape
their cage & I'm only concerned about blame.
I don't walk on the asphalt due to fear of bullets.

I stay in my lane, the one I am resigned to.
Forty-five acres & no mule, none of it
mine, none of it untouched by human
hands by now. I both desire & don't want

all of the knowledge of horrible histories,
the blood that the roots have felt & drank.
I sense something I can only call temporary,

something simultaneously gouged & gorgeous.
My presence here the duration of half a cycle
of the moon I can't find. I am making change
& thus am also changed—but for what?

Ryan Tito Gapelu

The pua and the plait

Fucking isn't like making lei / with lei can start over / take it all apart / use the same pieces / put her back together again

Can weave and unweave / pull and tug at the cords / resilient and pliable / she can take my calloused hands / and turn them beautiful

With lei you can run your fingers / through and around the curves / of the pua and the plait / an endless twirl / the very essence of her a god

Fucking feels like taking / like wrecking the softest grove / a delicately folded pulsing stone / cracked open and spilling / the magic out

I take the grove and the stone / the pua and the plait and swallow / her poli pulsing inside against mine / the grove murmuring against my chest / speaking heart to heart

What was I saying again?

Fucking is like making lei / with lei can start over / take it all apart / use the same pieces / put her back together again.

Moni Garcia

Our Spider Plant

every morning   he waters the plant hanging
from the only window in the dining room
its leaves   falter towards floor
& attempt to reach the color they mimic

looking out the only window   in the dining room
father ushers   winter's sunlight in
reaches for the yellow it lyrics
to save a plant i abandoned   thought dead

father tries to usher sunlight to his mouth
        a form of love he cannot sip
wants to save a sorrow   he abandoned dead
        & makes with his hands   a river

the love he wants to sip   tastes of loneliness
        his sister   halved from life / his heart
                he rivers into his hands
the grief he longs to break

                        his daughter   halved from his side
                i forget to call him   in the piercing of day
                        but father turns from his grief.   breaks
        into the heat of the dining room   to my plant

        where he cannot forget to call a piercing day
a morning   where the plant hangs and thirsts

through the dining room's heat & plants
his feet to the floor unfaltering. unleaving. until it drinks

Francis Gene-Rowe

Manic Pixie Mushroom and Her Extinct Goth Tree Girlfriend

I've whispered seventeen trees,
      now, each time
      their musty groan
      an exhalation of duration
      a release
            years upon years of
pollutants
           we're neither the disease
          nor the cure
there is no historicity, toxicity
           is a blank space, if space it
           can be called
They've never listened, except
really that means I really that means
we, if we can be called.
They're listened to, outside the walls
of borders of corpses of ever straightened
lines of degradation without decay
of ruins denied their own ruination
        poisoned and shattered to a wreckage
          labour without pay

I'd like
I'd really, like
I'd like to, really   I would like
          my desire isn't possible.
You'd prefer   what would you prefer.
          no, let's water our garden
If I inhale, prickled by dry grass,
          the insects softly insecting
It doesn't need to be a confinement
It can be a space
          our space   in between
          beetles, worms, gossamer, violets
          these are a few of my favourite names
          ripe with decaying life

          don't trouble, slough off your entire skin
          before the cruel sun of Today, malignantly
          dominant, burns it away. Stay close,
I'll press softly against you, beneath your
shade, in your lee. You, me, our friends
the microbes, here, now, formerly before,
not yet the not-yet. Mortar our glimpse
of such moments, but let the bricks be soft
and crumbling, so that foxes and other exceptions
to our chosen aesthetic can slip in and out. The
moss rusted, the rust mossed. A pool of
dank pond life/murkily reflecting/your macabre
beauty (it's good to teem, now and then), until
          enough of your fallen canopy
          exhausts the oxygenic capabilities
          of our small, small world

don't bother unlocking the gate, we're
beyond such things, really, if you think
about it, if you feel anything at all.
This is our last moment, I am

not here, you are not now. You were my
seventh, sometimes when moonlight splashes
sweetly, just so   I touch my hair in a way
that's carefully careless, hold my breath
as I briefly remember our time together.
dryness. I need things like you to be a part of
it, to share conversation/in the scarce greenways.
I grow on your ruin, hold you in my
living death, but I can live without you.
      Let's keep infesting each other, just for
      now, in this now we once had,
      our porous dream, for as long as I can stay.
      I miss you, and every other tree I've
      Loved. The world, extinct, forgets,
      but I'll remember in my own way a
short while, water the garden
      we once had.

June Gervais

Forty Rows of Rosemary

"Generally speaking, a little rosemary goes a long way. This is not one of those times."
—SAM SIFTON, "Roasted Potatoes with Onions and Rosemary,"
from his cookbook *See You on Sunday*

1   Generally speaking, a little rosemary goes
2   a long way. This is not one of those times.
3   Banckes's Herbal, 1525, says of rosemary
4   *Take the flowers thereof and make powder*
5   *thereof and binde it to thy right arme*
6   *in a linnen cloth and it shale make thee light*
7   *and merrie.* Sounds to me like witchery, but
8   this enticing *Light and merrie* —yes, please,
9   these. In October the crickets still trill for mates
10   and the tomato plants still swell with fruit
11   and the pineapple sage sprouts scarlet flowers
12   but three minutes into dinner, the sun pulls
13   an Irish goodbye. Let this be the year
14   I don't go with it. I'd submit to any conjuring.
15   Bathe and bind my whole body with rosemary.
16   Cull peppermint from the stone wall, chamomile
17   from the labyrinth, lavender from the boundary
18   markers. Gather coriander, even, in fistfuls
19   like a lover's hair: Answer the cold and dark
20   with citrus pique, medieval aphrodisiac.
21   Culpeper, 1653: *Hot in the first degree.*
22   Pliny, 1469: *Place it under the pillow before*
23   *sunrise.* I myself am little, and after equinox,
24   becoming littler, would go a long way for sunrise,

25   for a potent dose of green.
26   Culpeper on rosemary:
27   *The sun claims privilege in it, and it is under*
28   *he celestial Ram.* Culpeper says of its *chymical oil,*
29   *take one drop, two, three, as the case requires,*
30   *for inward griefs.* Culpeper says *Yet it must be*
31   *done with discretion, for it is very quick and piercing*
32   *and therefore a little must be taken at a time*
33   which is to say a little goes a long way
34   unless it is *one of those times,* as Sifton says.
35   When *sunrise* ceases to be a mild postcard word.
36   Becomes a word of piquancy *in the third degree*
37   because it means the sun will come. Will come
38   again *Light and merrie* just as the season comes
39   to take a quill to recipes. Red-pen *one drop*
40   and write in garden-green ink: *dispense freely.*

Paul Goudarzi-Fry

Saturated Ekphrases

—I

Settle, and blossom out my neck, prickly pear,
boy of the desert. Only the flowering. Keep your fruit.
Sand and sagebrush lizard will drink your inner waters.
Yes, a desert, but the plump body underneath withstands
what we think of you. What we imagine life to be.
Open your lips to the gossamer hummingbirds.
Drink, and be drunk. Bloom, and be marveled at.
When the body is eaten, only then allow withering.

—II

I still think they're too young to hold a cherry like that.
Still wonder how they would have chosen to go; could've
been me holding them like a cherry in the teeth, just barely,
just casting shadows of encouragement and half-truths.
Like a lion. No, an alligator, with a tall and squeak-filled
hatchling. From a cherry stone, they emerge, eyes closed,
and stilled—no, poised. A knowing smile of omnivore
teeth. For what else would I give my life?

—III

They wriggled out of their eggs and ate everything in sight
together. They're eating still. Or perhaps exploring a compound
hawkweed. We're all tired; let them regain their strength.
Aposematism gives them the edge. Don't you look away.

And don't imagine your tongue against those little black claws.
They'll tear you open and rest inside, caterpillars forever, soundly
wriggling and eating and not wondering what they would have
done if they were merely born butterflies.

— IV

The dickcissel cries in want of want, less sparseness, more
for a place in the world behind him. He is a juvenile. His
feet grasp firmly for this flight, although it is not his first time
warming himself in the summer. What an expanse, what an eye
that watches with twisting clicks, a warm-up before three direct
declamations; he can hear his unborn chicks overlaid. And
pause. He can always fly. Or he can stay here and turn his head
towards me, uncertainly. But then he twitches. Then he flies.

— V

What's the use of a kale leaf covering his bedenimed crotch.
Just out of frame, she might have been laughing. Still, too.
She held it up as new leaves grow, and his muscles flexed
outward, veins ridged and golden, far from farmer's tan border.
A perfect leaf, honored and embarrassed, above a weeded
audience. When the wind blew, you could hear the blades
clapping. Just before, he was so far from Adam. Just now,
his wife knows the revelation. Her shirt read: Moonchild.

— VI

Three magpies coax each other in distant croaks, I think,
or just hopping with authority. The sandstone opens to them
in a moment of no erosion. Rain's been gone for four years.
The canyon diffuses; or is diffused. Three magpies play in
light shadows. Animal play, a mark of intelligence. On the
fence, a magpie spoke to me, but his words were too close

to God. I forget if he joined the three magpies, together as
they picked the eyes from a doe, fallen from the high plateau.

—VII

You can't dive in, but the boats may motor through. You can't
swim, but there's nothing around but cicada song today.
Such an empty sky, but empty as in clean, as in, enough, a
touch of white clouds to kiss the earth another day. The ring
of emerald shoulders the pond. Young trees, loud as the wind.
At night, each bows and drinks with a hidden esophagus. This
morning shows where the rust-colored shallows vanish and
give way to the mild threats of nowhere, summer's nowhere.

—VIII

Greatness, in the vapor's inflorescence, seeding the water as
if fish could look upwards and envision, with uncertainty, heaven;
a breathless place that loses all its color when you accept it.
The setting sun bloomed through that night. We sat in the car
afterwards and smelled each other's skin from opposite seats.
In a parallel season, my body reveals every shade. In this, I honed
into the perfectly level layers of the earth, what was above earth.
I painted life over truth.

Rhienna Renée Guedry

Our gardens are just environments we pretend to control

So instead of another panic
attack I repot the plant whose
     fibers &   roots need more
space   I borrow good
soil from two pots, I put my   hands in
dirt   my hands
          around the shoulders
          of roots   like
life, like death,

Like rescue   I want to move   earth
objects   want something   to do   with my hands to
keep them from shaking   but it is more than that
          I need something to
          thrive if we aren't, so dirt
spills out on the
                    counter & the floor, it gives me
                    purpose   to clean the   mess
I made   my own damn self

&   on the parcel of land
where I hover, I eat, I sleep & plant into
                    I think
          about   which plants will

       survive   despite my intervention how
some fruit craves neglect   &some
seeds   erupt in garbage

    & yet someone on the internet
asserts that   piss *provides an excellent source of*
       nitrogen, phosphorous, potassium & trace elements for plants
      Ain't that the way
   drill for oil   destroy a coastline
      blow up a levee   save one mansion
Piss on a garden bed, *it is nourishment*
I am helping

Jo Güstin

Letter to Rihanna

My dearest Rihanna,
It is me,
Maman,
And 3 AM in Montreal.
I am writing to you in English because I am not sure at this point, that you
    would pardon my French
The language of my *"je t'aime"*
And all the words I sang to you
In that bedroom,
Those other ones,
On the front seat of a U-Haul,
Or when you were in my backpack
While I was riding Ruth Ryders
The old bicycle taking us
All to a place I thought was home.

It never was, I am sorry.
I had to move out all the time
Holding you tight
Scared and weary,
Kissing your leaves
To give me strength . . .
The tear stains on my badass shades
Looked like the bars of a prison
The ones denying you freedom
Not the ones serving you cocktails.

My dearest dearest Rihanna
Maman suffocates in her guilt
I haven't seen you in a while,
As weeks and weeks and months go by
I just keep breaking my promise
That "take care" song behind your name
I meant every word, I promise
I've never loved so constantly
You're the one who took care of me

My sweet baby, I feel ashamed
I need a home to be your mom
And I struggle with permanence
In a country so hard to love
Where nobody ever loved me
I thought I'd have found it by now
By the time I turned 35
You wouldn't be my single child
You'd thrive in a forest of love

You were my practice of caring
For someone other than myself
And of building a family
Some pets, some plants, a wife maybe
I was told you would never die
That's one thing we had in common
Snake plants *are* great for a first time
You forgave all my oversights

Will you forgive me for failing
At my one job of raising you?
I will forgive you for loving
Your plant-sitter much more than me.
He is the best, I'll give you that
And the best choice I've ever made

He has the home, the plants, the wife,
My vision board? That's just his life.

When we reunite I will have
A beautiful home of my own
What if I'm sick of "Canada"?
What if I am forever gone?
What if I've been gone all this time
Like a phantom in denial?
I'll have to stop being your mom
I will have to break my own heart.

Are you waiting, my Rihanna?
Are you waiting for my return?
I am in Montreal right now,
But yesterday it was Berlin and tomorrow, back in Paris,
Then maybe, *maybe* Wellington.
Don't you think I am having fun
Being a stranger everywhere!
I'm trying to find the right pot
When there's no earth for the Black queer

Top Ten favorite places in los angeles

welcome, & unlock thousands of heartwarming savings. the boba time on vermont & the one on vermont again, little further down, across from ________ ___________. menu covered in dancing skeletons, sit down and experience 3x the nirvana. bogo cup deal for officers on horseback. free upgrade to power. hi again, check out our properties. we're located in the backwash of twin octagon jails and the slap of jalapeño dough on bleach countertops, glisten, wetzel pretzel potential of an orange morning in the station. we never close. coffee in the station pitcher burning its own tongue over an over. skip town. double decker cars skate rubble, railroad spikes eat whole neighborhoods for breakfast. (step on in a filched village, off in santa fe.) before you go—don't miss aladdin bail bonds. the staff was so amazing. they work with you & try their very best to help you get your loved one out of jail quick.

then there's this deal where you can bite off more than you can chew. get hip to it. crouch down in thai basil grown from the light of helicopters. yam leaf lessons learned quick. garden glazed in carbon monoxide, formaldehyde, benzene, nitric oxide, soot. pluck from the main root, rat labyrinth where the rats play tag, stems covered in ant families, aunts and uncles carrying signals, signals bout a new crumb, back to the queen. carry legs, threads, and heart-shaped bites of leaves. while we're at it. don't miss pw liberationissweet1957* plus roaming Stater's for Strawberries at 11 pm on Valentimes Day : Wake up an smell thee..day oldfolger's teabag brewing in yer yellow cup. trying to undo the crick in our neck. crick in our whole life. that brittle searing shoulder blade from too much use. let's pour a gallon jug of vinegar from the gas station over the intersection of hill and college. replay the part where the tracks hoot

you way up the hill. feel the last twenty days blow through you. shape of your-
story not far from the shapeofyourmouth, swallowing over an over the road.

feeling crowded? take everything out. bring back only what you need

narinda heng

planting

My parents' hands
understand something
about making paradise
that mine are still
trying to figure out.

They've coaxed
growth from tiny seeds
and hard earth, brought
forth colors from brown dirt
in the form of green leaves,
red, yellow, orange fruit,
vegetables whose
English names I still
haven't figured out.

There was a year
when the whole rear
of the yard hosted
home-grown corn

there's still a patch
of sugarcane in the
corner behind the
makrut lime tree

they planted
dragonfruit just

to see if they could
(it grew)

it took years, but the
cherimoya trees now
bear heavy, juicy
bounty—my favorite.

My grandmother would
wistfully keep mango and
longan seeds, sprout them
in old cans, discarded paper cups,
then plant them, hoping
they'd somehow take to the
less than ideal climate,
find what they needed
in the unfamiliar soil.

After ten years, one
small mango sapling
still survived, bearing the
tiniest mangos I'd ever seen

it made us all giggle,
this tree holding on
so valiantly to life and
putting forth all it could.

Somehow they turned
their modest plot of land
in Santa Ana into a
lush bit of Cambodia

I remember sitting on
the roof one day
and looking over

the tops of the trees
and thinking that
I could almost forget
what country I was in.

My parents—their hands
have a habit of making
paradise wherever there is
a patch of dirt and a hose

I used to wish they'd get
rid of a tree or two, dig up
the yard, put in a swimming pool

I'm glad they never did.

I understand now
that they were never
trying to make paradise

they were making
home.

Marcy Rae Henry

Los saguaros are being destroyed

The sun is needed and also dangerous
Beneath it people hide things for others
en la sombra de saguaros

Water in containers painted black
to absorb not reflect sun
Sunscreen   Sombreros
Clothes   Crude maps

Imagine the sun betraying your whereabouts
Not using a phone for fear
of becoming a little black
dot crossing a line
.   .   .   .
Oh sí, your location is being commodified
Along with cages and the cages around them

A   virus   travels   like   the   rich

Saguaros can die of frost
spreading over expandable skin and fruit red as royalty

Wooden ribs can hold two hundred gallons of rain
Si se dejan al sol y la lluvia saguaros can live two centuries
As long as this country has been
Longer than this f r o n t e r a has been

                              To kill or steal a saguaro is a felony

          Cactus cops normalmente roam the border
now stand by while saguaros are removed
                    to make room for a wall whose removal
                          will be reminiscent of Berlin

Después de cien años a saguaro starts to grow its first arm
        lifting it into the sky as if to say
Dame tus cansados tus pobres your huddled masses
yearning to breathe libres   Envíame los desposeidos
    I lift my lámpara beside the sun-colored door

KateLynn Hibbard

Unblossoming

*

at the last open flower market in LA,
at the peak of the pandemic,
a photographer buys dozens of flowers —
lilies, roses, carnations, freesia —
to document their *slow entropic unblossoming*
which is another way to say death,
as days turned into weeks and weeks into
you know how the rest of this story goes

*

senescence: not to bloom
                              flower   open   unfold
                   develop   mature
but fade

not to progress
                              evolve   flourish   thrive
                   prosper   burgeon
but decline

*

To extend the life of cut flowers,
add sugar salt copper pennies vinegar aspirin bleach

*

There is nothing living which does not breathe nor anything breathing which does not live.

*

The unperturbed adult lung is remarkably quiescent

*

When does the body leave the room?
When does the person, the being, leave
the body? Why does the body persist,
and why do we sanction its persistence?
When my brain shuts down,
have I left my body? When I fall asleep,
have I left my body? Where
did I leave it? Where does the brain go
when the body is at rest?

*

While still in the womb, the lungs grow like a tree from a bud, with branches sprouting from left and right trunks.

*

Did you wait too long to quit smoking?
Was that asbestos wrapped around the furnace pipes?
Did you grow up on a farm, inhaling with pleasure
late summer air hazy with particulate matter
while your father harvested grain?

*

Church	*in regards to the no-property theory, the dead body was under the control of the*
Corpse	*The term synonymous to a dead body is*
Common Law	*the major source of mortuary law is*
Cadaver	*A dead human body used for anatomical study is a*
Decomposition	*The most positive sign of death is*
Decent Burial	*The law states that every person has a right to a*
Mutilation	*Embalming is a form of*
Quasi-property	*A dead human body is said to be*
Dead human body	*is not property in a real sense*
Surviving Spouse	*As a rule, the right of decent disposal belongs to the*

*

did you actually mean unblushing or unpleasing?

*

A cut flower cannot take on nutrients
so it slowly begins to die, though putting it in water
can lengthen its life. Disturbing the flow of water
shortens life. Cutting flowers in the air
instead of under water
may produce bubbles.
Bent neck.
Quick wilt.

*

Aren't we all going to die of something? Well?

Nora Hikari

Exposition on Pears,
as a Transmisogynist

You, too, could hate pears
if you tried. You too could pick
a hatred—plump, meat-soft,
cloying, overly-earnest—
if you reached high enough.

They're just not the right shape.
Fruit comes in shapes. Fruit comes
in rounds and oblongs
and delicate teardrop ruby cuts.
What shape is a pear? What is "pear-shaped?"
What audacity, named after itself.

A pear is too eager to be cut.
Nothing gives the way a pear does.
Gives and gives and gives and for what?
To be bright and mild and of teeth?
Nothing should want to yield
like that. To be so simple,
not even to be cut, but
like dancing, like back-leading,
the hint of a cut, the intonation
of a request, and the pear
falls apart. What a gimmick.

Where is the tartness? The way
the flesh should cleave sharp and tight?
Nothing but sweet and grain and give.
Cain himself kept
the pear for himself, knowing
nothing about it was harsh,
which is all that God beckons outward.

No, a pear is a failure. A pear
wants something it shouldn't have,
which is for you to love it,
even though it is easy,
because it is soft,
because it asks,
and because it is all
it has ever wanted.

Ellie Howard

Seedbombing a Golf Course

A pine walking-bridge traces the country club fairways
like a nervous finger on a hem. Above the wetland,
I watch the men pared to a pendulum,
their golf carts fixed around buzzcut lawns.

Laborers trim the greens on even-numbered days,
brush and sterilize the bunkers weekly.
White polos and ironed khakis patter
about the manicured grass.

I glide across the sidelong path each day,
considering the best-suited plants
to seed along the fairway—succulents for the sand,
shallow-rooted crops for the putting greens.

Beside the course, briars deluge the sinking marsh
like blackberry bushes snaring my childhood home.
The irrigation systems are robust.
A few of the lakes are shallow enough

for a paddy field, the deeper waters
could be stocked with fish. The men spurn
the hazards that creep into their argyle socks.
I worry that I will always be this:

A container for play outlined by men,
unnatured, defertile trap,

set of holes, *no trespassing* nailed to an oak.
A view from the balconies edging the boardwalk.

Talicha J.

Another Year Sprouts

eager to   unfold.
every goal i made for the last one
                              wilted,
the walking pad and dumbbells collected
dust & dog fur, the bank accounts   withered and decayed,
the unwatered plant purchased on a whim
                                   browned
on the side table beneath the lamp.
i was selfish,   hungry   for aesthetics, to be   a plant girlie.
snapping photos with a filter while my first philodendron birkin
         dried up.   i did not know how or even if i *could*
save it,   i barely tried.
tossed it in the trash,
                    decorative pot and all.

Umang Kalra

REMEMBER WHEN THEY TOLD US THE MUSHROOMS COULD TALK

to each other & here   we were wondering what they would say to us. I am wondering what they'd think of bipolar disorder in their limited vocabulary. I am wondering if they know   what a funeral is. Consider sunset: surely they know the absence of vitality,   surely they touch each other at nighttime too, surely   they know what I'm talking about when I name lust a problematic emotion. Consider rain: do they know they are drinking it? At the end of the next apocalypse when all the people are gone, will the internet try to kill everything else? What do   the mushrooms think? Do they want to live? Do they know what an evolutionary instinct is? What do we do with all this capitalism, so deep   that we are surveilling   the fungus. Picture the afterlife: intelligence is only artificial   when the people who made it   are still alive / intelligence is a construct of humanness / mushrooms will probably exist long   after we do. Picture the afterlife: the wires have taken over   our buildings and cities, roots crawling   over their crevices, the mushrooms   using their 50 "words" to tell them it's okay   that they lived   despite us.

Esmé Kaplan-Kinsey

the office // the after

my office one thousand feet in the sky
my cube of nothing one thousand
feet in the sky with the potted orchid
in the corner that blooms violently
pink twice a year, budget blossoms
because HR says: studies show
the presence of plants is soothing
to clients and hey, I like them too,
I'm not complaining, just drinking
coffee metallic-black every faded morning
waiting for the pigeons that shit
daily on my windowsill, come flurrying
in gray and green and black and white
and I can't tell them apart, any more
than they can distinguish me
from every other gravity-defying ape
in this forest of glass —
and on some long overtime evenings I wonder:
this interchangeability: deliberate?
this soft insistent signaling:
the eggshell walls, fluorescence,
the calculated asymmetry
the caffeine on tap the mirrored
mountain or seashore or rolling gold
quick-shifting plain of the screensaver
these murmurs get me forgetting
if I was ever given a name —
the air conditioning's scent is called

Mountain Evergreen and it smells like nothing
that has ever existed, but on mornings
when I come into the office early
its spice unlatches a truth, of a sort:
I was here before the falling-apart. I swear,
I remember how the starlings on the telephone wires
dotted out the notes to some atonal song
and there were fish then, great clouds of them
drifting green-silver through the dark
of the lake and one summer I walked barefoot
in the grassy ditch along a gravel road
until my heels bled grasshoppers flinging
themselves against my ankles heat shimmering
off the earth like fish swimming
through the air red-tailed hawks
watching silent from the fence-posts —
these are the things I remember now,
when I think back to before they mattered —
there were fruits in the forest then,
salmonberries, pink-blooming plums,
the domed red heads of mushrooms pushing
through the leaf litter and sometimes,
on the luckiest of nights, I'd stand in the air,
just out in the clean evening air,
and watch the starlings vortex upwards
in a single inhale.

Mukethe Kawinzi

woman

i would have told her
ceanothus blueblossomed
overnight, except

slow is how we are taking it,
slow as siltstone sets, slow as spring
lambs slogging through bush,
slow, as a banana slug might
slide through sprouted yarrow.

every poppy i passed today
was open, i wanted to tell her,

to ask, how gold does trefoil
come in outside your terrace,

how many monarchs mounting
sun cup did you count, did pink

petal, did balm of heaven
make it down your throat?

i would have, except

she named the plants after her exes.

She told me she was a cultivator first, a lover second, and maybe that's why she always preferred flowers over chocolates as a gift. In her over-two-decades' worth of existence on Earth, she never had a relationship last longer than the cut flowers her dates would give her. Except one, we both supposed.

Her apartment was populated with plants—all grown with the care and affection she never gave their namesakes. I asked her if she planned on naming one after me. She smiled then; lips crooked, eyes twinkling, as if she already had a list in her head of which genera of succulent matched my jawline.

The Burro's Tail that hung above the television was named Aria. They met at a yard sale. Aria had eyes like mine: dark brown and dangerously astute. They bonded over Aria's fascination with classic horror films. Each 5-star review on her letterboxd was attached to a faux documentary that bordered on snuff, and their last date was spent watching a man's abdomen get inverted. She bought the Burro's Tail from the same yard sale she snatched up Aria, and she told me on my first visit to her apartment that if I tried hard enough, I could smell blood on its leaves.

An Aloe Vera named Katie sat in the kitchen, picked apart and miserable. I learned its name after burning my hand on the electric stove. Katie was beautiful, kind. Her voice lulled people to be just as gentle. She was nothing med school valued. Their lives became intertwined in a waiting room. Katie was hungry for an excuse to change her career path. She was hunting for a fool soft enough to cut open. Her memory had been bad since childhood, but she began to learn—don't have unsafe sex, turn off the stove when not in use, water the Aloe Vera, and don't expect a lover to do the same.

In the bedroom, Ginger the Eve's Needle reminded her every night that some people bloomed faster than plants. Ginger realized he was a man after their first and only night together. She barely considered him an ex. After our first night together, I told her that Ginger was a cactus, not a succulent. She said that every label a botanist gave a plant was fake, and that she was not exclusionary when it came to her love of plants. Though, she did have her preferences.

It was hard not to remember them all. Each of their terracotta pots were labeled. The only nameless one was the most recent—a Jade Plant that she rescued from the family moving out of 14B. Its leaves were already shriveling. I knew from what she had told me that it was in need of something. From her, I knew which camera tricks Burro's Tails considered cheap scares, which chemical compounds Aloe Veras always mixed up on their practice tests, and how scared Eve's Needles looked when they realized they made a mistake. And I knew she was a cultivator first and a lover second, but I never knew her name. I knew *Aria*, and *Katie*, and *Ginger*, and *Jez*, and *Casey*, and *Levi*, and all their botanical nomenclature. She kept her own name out of sight, never uttered or penned down inside the apartment walls, because after all these years, she must have realized there was nothing more intimate and more dangerous to give someone than her name.

I told her I was a writer. She asked me if I planned on writing about her.

Rebecca Kinkade-Black

Plantcestors

Aren't we all just seeds to start?
Seeds planted in the eyes of our creator
Progenitor of our existence
Is that why we feel kinship
with our plantcestors?
Deeply rooted in kéyah
we develop limbs and leaves
and systems of connection
We, too, become life bringers
of thoughts and ideas
of kindness and community
sometimes of biological kin
"We are all connected"
is not just some trite phrase
It is remembrance
that we are all unified
by the molecules that make us
You, me, and the tree

Tara Labovich

[A TOMATO IS A GASP]

a tomato is a gasp
in the leaves.
a succulent, a prayer
in a sheaf.
in the august garden
the reaching for hvn
never stops, it's been built
into me. i heard once
that the point
of life is pain.
a shadow,
the darkening
carving out the edge of de-
light—carving,
into the nectarean, like tomato
juice carves green'd
rivers down my arm
when i bite,
how i shiver,
how the cold
spoons the heat.

BEE LB

ode to each life within sightline

kalanchoe pumila—o flower dust,
your soft grey body stretching and
stretching and curling and weaving.

o, you poor sundrenched thing.
you would push your way through
the window if it were possible, and i'd let you.

i'd watch your trailing arms curve through the grass,
put down roots in endless soil, grow as far as you can
reach. but come winter, you'd wither, if you made it past

fall. so i will let your body lean this way and that,
perpetually stuck in your sway, body growing taller,
an unmoving dance to music that settles your dust.

heartleaf philodendron—o heartleaf,
forgive me for thinking you pothos
at first. surely you know your own name.

the second my mistake was pointed out,
you shot up, nearly a dozen coiled leaves encased in—
what is it you encase your new growth in? all i see is film,

in time turned gold and dropped as a husk.
o philodendron, forgive me naming you frank.
forgive me calling you leggy. forgive me constantly

trying to teach you to vine. i am not unconvinced
you'll never learn. at the least, you'll get more sun
pinned to the length of the window than trailing the table's top.

tradescantia zebrina—o zebrina, forgive me as well,
another mistaken identity. to be fair, in the harsh light
your purple wasn't so vibrant as to stand apart.

your leaves covered in peachfuzz, i thought gave you away.
o inch plant, forgive me trying to give you away. i wanted
a teddy bear vine, and each of your pointed tips led towards

the wrong conclusion. i did not want the association
of your most common name, did not want to call you dude,
did not want you to die in my mother's hands.

you may still die in mine, we'll see. your longest vines
fell, now arranged a faux-bouquet in water,
the smallest of roots growing each day.

dracaena trifasciata—o snake plant, you know
i'm trying my best. we both know you're only here
because you cost next to nothing, but i promise,

i'm doing my best to revive you. i'll admit,
i've already failed once. let one stalk turn to mush
in my rush to water, then let it crisp in my days away.

o mother-in-law's tongue, i'll cut it off once i'm sure
you'll survive. til then, i'll let it be the closest to the sun,
keep the rest of your foliage from scorching. i'll admit,

i'd like to hurry you along. like to cut your chopped stalk
at the base, see if i can get more of you to take. your endearing
v-cuts so you root right way up. how long will you take to settle in?

i'll assume we're both counting the hours of sun.

kalanchoe fedtschenkoi — o lavender scallops, do you know
how long i avoided you? your name brought to mind sliced starch
or the chewiest tasteless orbs. neither held much draw

in the form of a plant. but you are a smoother version
of my flower dust, and when the small body began putting out roots
in water, i wanted a pair to pot it with, and there you were

if not a twin, a close cousin, the red lining each of your edges
not far from the purple of their base. i can admit, the propagated pair
didn't take, but you alone have pushed out aerial roots,

one already curling down your pot, the others standing straight,
pink-tipped, the newest; a pair of twins. o kalanchoe, o stonecrop,
none of your names fit you, but i'm glad to call you mine.

ceropegia woodii variegata — o string of hearts, my first love,
the introduction to my latest obsession. you came to me
in a pot the size of my thumb, found after four phone calls

and something like forty minutes pouring over the smallest
selection to pick the perfect plant. you with your pink flare,
your green splash, your vines curling like string.

the moss in your soil didn't last, but the clovers have kept growing
for nearly a year now. from green to purple to pink to yellow
and then a new patch coming back again. o rosary vine, i promise,

in time, i'll let you trail. but for now i'll keep you piled on the windowsill,
untangle your tendrils every few days, let the light seep into
your waiting body. o sweetheart vine, how you've grown for me.

how wide your hearts have gotten.
how much growth you've yet to give.

Jessica Le

The fact that green beans grow like two meters tall

in the house across
from my parents' backyard
or that it took two hours
to find that stepladder
or ladder, whatever
you call it, to prop up
against that old fence.
I looked into the green beans
my neighbour planted.
Then I took my hat off
and let the heat
look into my back.
Thought, why the hell
are there so many green beans?
I stared hard until the cat came,
and waved to my neighbour,
who, after a moment, waved back,
startled, and I laughed, thinking
of how touching
the hot chin of a stray cat
startles anyone, because
that hard hollow triangle of bone
kissing your hand
never gets old, no matter what.

Nolan Lee

Irises

I

His first visit to the art gallery deserves no remembrance except that he glanced at the photograph of the irises (Irises) on his way out, and that this was his first encounter with them.

II

Compelled by something unknown, he visited the gallery again. This visit, he stood before the irises for about thirty seconds, noting the symmetry of the titular flowers, the straightness of their stems, and the blocky patches of shine on the vase. That is the extent of what he noticed, but his noticing was admirable for a person. Again, the flowers were the last piece he observed.

III

This visit lasted for two minutes. That morning's fresh sun had opened his mind to clarity, and he knew he'd not given the irises their fair due. He learned them to be the work of Robert Mapplethorpe, so he fastidiously studied the photograph for perversion. The irises were phallic and the vase yonic, or the irises yonic and the vase phallic. He attempted to see both the irises and the vase as phallic, wanting to entertain Mapplethorpe's androphilia, but could not, at that point. He dreamed of the irises in their gilded black and white, that night.

IV

He only read the description of the irises once, because their description angered him. He would have vocalized his disturbance, but found he could not indulge sound. He instead narrowed his sight to the irises alone while banishing his other senses. The curator or someone had connected the temporary beauty of flowers to the temporary beauty of people, specifically those poor victims of the AIDS epidemic. He disliked on principle that humans would think of themselves as relevant to irises, the idea that their preoccupation with meaning had anything to do with the irises, which had nothing to do with any person. He reached his hand out towards the flowers, wanting to feel their skin under his fingers, but was gently led out by a guard, which he disliked on principle.

V

This visit he came to view only the irises, swatting away birds and insects on his journey to the gallery. He picked a feather from his hair. (His trip had been treacherous.) He planted himself before the irises, swaying gently in the gallery's ambient air currents. He noticed that the petals ascended an angular matterhorn of light formed by the sun penetrating some out of frame windows, that the shadow of the irises in the bottom left corner was like the shadow of a bushy and vital tree, and that the photograph would make a lovely still life, yes, by some Impressionist master, but had already achieved perfection in simply being the irises themselves. He was in front of the irises for many hours.

VI

This visit he picked petals out of his hair as well, circled by a confusion of bees, arriving at the gallery at the moment of its opening. The inside of his mouth tasted sweet. A woman who looked like Diane Arbus had photographed him on the walk. He did have some idea of what was happening.

He neglected noticing the unevenness of light on the vase, or the shadow cast on the right side of the wall behind the irises, or photography, because those things had become frightening. He had had a job, yes, but by then he didn't much care about how to reach it, and so he spent the whole of his day with the irises. He realized he was in the gallery, and not looking out at the gallery, after some time, and left once he was required to.

The irises did not stay and they did not leave.

He would have left bed to visit the irises again, but he did not have to. He was not in bed. A rush of nonspecific bloom was seeping out of his mattress and searching for chinks in the loam of its foam chunks, from which old hairs were being expelled.

j marvain

in conversation with orchids

i keep running fingertips
along the sunflower of my skin
like a path,
                        or an exit
forgive me if ever i follow the stem

tracing lines to exhale —
if for a moment
ponds of dewdrops blossoming pink
i had such steady hands painting forests
i don't know what
changed

gnashed and shattered leaves
are changed too, though,
seasons make sure of that
winter strips each orchid to a memory
year over
                        year
but for all of the wreckage that lays
on that path,
there is a promise of petals
returning again
this fragile body is bare
                        but it will be pink

forgive me—
some chemical blight
will always look to the stem
and imagine how it feels
to greet earth at its root
i do not know where the years will find me
or if the seasons will steady their hands
enough to grasp that life is
                    and will be
perennial

celina mcmanus

bog baby

a transidyll

bog baby, you have become the tamarack. are you there, bog baby? bog baby, i am not sure how to swim through the tentacles. bog baby, i am here for you. i see you under there, slimy and giggling. bog baby, let me tell you a story. once, i was just like you. only, i was enshrined in an american sycamore. she monkey-barred my whole body until i found what skin can feel like outside of human sway. she fed me small fingers of sap and whirligigs. back then i called them helicopters, but isn't *whirligigs* much nicer? there's less possible violence in it. and why is there violence attached to a seed? not all winged things slice. when seeds take flight, they have only growth in mind: tower there, tower here, whispers of coupling in an underground internet of roots. bog baby, have you ever met a violent maple? i'm wondering now, if there is any such thing as neutrality? oh, bog baby, don't cry, i'll tell you sweet secrets from now on. like how i found myself on an island not meant for me, swimming with humpbacks. how i tasted the crackle of okra on my tongue that traveled over stolen seas . . . here i go again, twisting the root until it breaks. wait, i think i've finally got you free. what is it now? why are you squirming toward the bog again? why, you didn't want to be freed at all. you were already free, weren't you?

Rita Mookerjee

Cardboard Cutout Palm Tree

While you're horizontal on canvas furniture that
doesn't look the way it did in the catalog, slick can in hand
cold condensation, you're supposed to say *this is the
life* when really you should be asking *is this my life*

because at what point do muscled cabana boys and
flower-tending boys and cocktail-serving boys
become one tan, tropical amalgam, interchangeable
at each location, and everyone wears that goddamn print,

the hibiscus with its showy pistil jutting out like a penis
like a magic wand pointing you to the sample area
where they're offering piña colada espresso shots
appealing to your desire to stockpile mini umbrellas

and antioxidants because these are the things that
you prioritize in Florida. You gulp the shot, and
think that it's the pick me up you've been missing
but when you brew it at home, the stuff tastes like mud

and baby powder, so you toss the whole cannister
in the garbage and open the floral encyclopedia
that hurts your wrists to hold.
you look up hibiscus anatomy, stupid fucking

flower that it is, and you wonder why people don't
favor the pitcher plant or nightshade or gloxinia,
which you read is a greenhouse plant so it isn't
in the nursery with its paved trails painted green

in a bad impression of grass, sprinkled with retired people
who realized too late that they didn't have any hobbies.

Tiffany Morris

saguaro, at sunset

half-buried in orange sand
the wind-carved wood
remembers its cactus skin,
its blossomed breath —
each petal a jewel
plucked from its crown
in flashes of bright plumage —
days measured in
rustling phantoms,
the sky itself a song.

Sreeja Naskar

she left in autumn and everything i've planted since has grown teeth

the tomatoes refuse to ripen without her breath in the kitchen / the mint turned bitter the day her toothbrush dried / i told myself i could grow past her / that i could bury the memory like compost / something holy in decay / but every time i dig a hole for something new / i hit the bones of what she left / her hair still wrapped in the roots / her laughter caught in the wind-chime parsley / she kissed me with lips that were thyme and absence / said she loved me like wild things love fire / desperate / doomed / i kept her letters in the freezer, thought cold might preserve goodbye better than heat / the rosemary grew sideways after she left, crooked toward the emptiness / i pruned it and bled / i bled into the soil until the basil grew red-veined / everything in this garden knows her / the vines curl like her wrists / the sunflowers tilt like her head when she lied / i water them anyway / i tell them nothing is wrong / but they bloom too fast / then wilt too soon / like they're reenacting the part where she said forever and meant tuesday / grief has a scent / it's damp earth and sour lavender / it's a hand pulling the roots before the flower opens / it's the way i still plant things i know won't live / just to feel something die in my hands that isn't her.

Miriam Navarro Prieto

Borago Officinalis as Pleasure

A year passed of you picking me up from class, every Friday,
you waited for me outside, with your six-years-older-than-me pose,
We walked to my mother's home, had lunch together, took a nap,
and I always complied, thought myself full enough just because you were.
But that springtime afternoon, my hungry hand caught by accident
what had always been between my light green sheets, climbing
up my calves: unexpected scent of chlorophyll, the warmest
flash of indigo coming up my thighs. Yes. I still don't know how
I came to the conclusion that the best thing I could do for myself
was grabbing you and use you. Yes. Stamens covering my eyes blind
but never stop my hand. Yes. There. Sweet nothingness. For the first time
I arrived at my destination, seventeen, starflowers flooding my mattress,
a stupid boyfriend panicking. We lasted another year, exclusively thanks
to my hand learning how to use your otherwise trivial manliness.
Thank you. Yes.

Nnenna Loveth Umelo Uzoma Nwafor

Self-Disguise as a Cactus
[2021]

I get all my nourishment from myself.

(I'm sooo chill!)

When you're not looking,
I satiate my thirst
and longing by looking
for you in the sun.

(I barely need any water!)

I drink all the dregs from the air
and soil. *(You can forget about me
for weeks!)* I parch everything
in my appetite for a sweet watering.

It still won't be enough.
I hold on to every drop for a dryness
that I know will inevitably come again
until the next time you come again.

I love you regardless.
Seem content.
Pretty. Vibrant.
Thick green skin.
What a glow! you'll say.

I'll survive. I'll be here *(no pressure!)*
You can come back
when you can *(and that means*
you'll always come back!)
But when you water me?
I can burst into a bloom.

When the care comes, with some consistency
I know it's safe to spare some energy
for this pink indulgence of a heart.

AJ O'Reilly

Very Old Trees

There's a line of great big redwoods behind my tiny house in Portland that I think of as my grandfathers, and when the wind blows really hard as it does more and more often in the age of climate crisis branches, big branches, are prone to crack off and fall (in fact an entire tree broke in half and fell into the church parking lot behind me this winter, I see the three-story tall stump out my window every morning when I eat oatmeal, it has birds in it, and is growing new branches), and one of these redwoods spreads right above the skylight in the little loft where I sleep every night and so really it's just a matter of time until one of the branches falls on the roof of my house in a storm and maybe it cracks the glass and maybe the cracked glass and the cracked branches will fall into the house on me soon, I don't know, although I can tell you the storms are thrilling and I lay in bed and smile like a wizened ship's captain as the wind buffets my house about, but what I do know is that the last time we were in the redwoods in California it was me and my parents—I had rented a van and driven there to camp with them, an echo of the trip we used to take every summer when we were kids, there were a whole bunch of families and children running around then but this summer it was just my parents (who still go every year for their anniversary, it will be their 50th when they go next year) and me, not yet out to them as a queerdo, but (I would later learn) giving it away to them loudly with my rented van and my overalls and my extremely short new hair—my mom still won't stop talking about how surprised she is at the short showers I take these days when I took such long ones as a kid, and well, I don't know what to tell you mom, there's a lot of unnecessary labor I've given up on these days—but they were so happy and so proud to see me and so relaxed in that specific way they are when they're camping in the redwoods, and so there I was in the redwoods with my parents and they took me on the walk we used to go on as kids, the walk that takes you to the very old trees, I mean they are some of the oldest redwoods that there are which makes them some of the oldest trees that there are and they're just right there next to this state park campsite that I didn't exactly take for granted as a kid, I mean I knew it was extremely special, but it was also a part of my normal life and it's not now and often I won't go with my parents on the summer trip because they don't seem to mind breathing wildfire smoke and there's usually wildfire smoke and I mind it a lot in both my mind and my lungs, but it wasn't smoky this year and so I rented the van and came to the redwoods and I went with my parents on the walk on the way to the old trees in my overalls and my short short hair, and at one point they stopped, my 80 year old dad who still hikes every day and my 74 year old mom whose hair literally still isn't gray, they stopped, and they pointed to a certain tree, and they said, "This is the tree that we want you to sprinkle our ashes under when we die"—and I nodded, and I looked down (sorel, sword ferns) and I looked up, and remembered the very old trees are so tall that the forest where they live contains three separate biomes, and there are creatures (like flying squirrels) that live in the upper story that we will never see in the understory and right then I felt very glad to know that there is room for the skylight and the wind and the smoke and the van and my hair and my parents and their ashes all at once.

J. C. Otiono

looking for a soft place to land

Love when met has little opportunity to become grief,
and I took to burying my grief beneath the soil.

I followed you:
succumbed to the hushed grove.
Those hands, so dark and beckoning
picked at the wound
and lulled me stuck
in amber and honey.

Let time
split yourself in two,
layers peeling away.
You pull at yourself slowly
until you are free.

Flattened into dirt,
how do I keep the leaves from curling?
I took to watering my grief,
for the rainwater to gather
for the soil to suck
most, where it hurts.

Rained upon the aching grin,
caught at half-gasp, half-kiss
in horrid warning:
Pull me in, pull me in.

I can't forget that
rouge has a taste,
a taste for the dead and near dying.

Let time
wrest tenderness from
my nosy pry of wet fingers,
throwing head back,
trying to fit lips around
the dreadful chase.
Bring to mouth the meat exposed;
let grief wrap her gums
its uneven pockmark of teeth
around its body
and sink them.

Saliva-slick melts
entrails when they kiss
slurping up, taking
without asking.

(All the soft places to land
have been sucked up)

And leaves behind,
a lonesome husk;
a lovely
laced up
candied treat.

In time,
I took to raising oneself up,
and looked again. I turn
to tongue the sunlight.

The Venus flytrap
from it's stitched-mouth modest
dares, too,
emerge with a grin.

Let love be at the end
Of this new, violent flowering.

Rituja Patil

Elegy

All I ever wanted was to cultivate cherry tomatoes with you. Mix
the coarse sand with diatomaceous earth and vermicompost. Put
some dry moss at the bottom of a plastic pot. We could've soaked
the cocopeat brick overnight. I wanted to break it with you.
The trouble is, I just cannot forget you. The memory begins and ends
at the same place—had I given the seed time, would it have grown to be
four feet tall? Would it then have chains upon chains of cherry tomatoes?
Would we then pluck them together? What kind of baskets
would we pick them in? Would we then eat them? Would they be juicy,
tart and crisp? Would you make sourdough bread and put flaxseeds on it?
Would I drain the cottage cheese with a muslin cloth? Would we drink buttermilk?
Would I feed you with shaky hands and heart that beats like a wedding procession?
Would my lips part in unison with yours? The memory begins and ends at the same
place. The reach across the table leaves me empty handed. Would we have cultivated
a garden together, my darling? Would it have blossomed and dried up as we aged?

Isaac Pickell

The scientific name for someone I used to know

I write to your memory from the peak
of a warm summer rainstorm that soaks
the day, making it gloomy yet somehow
becoming, like the chorus of a broken

social scene song. It's really coming down,
from bright grey skies that hide the high
noon sun, so hard it might flood the great big
pots we leave on the back deck. So I brave

the rain to check on them, and that's when I see
something that sounds your traces in the back of
my head: I want to write a poem, but I can't think
of any pretty ways to say the puckering at the heart

of my split-leaf philodendron reminds me of you.
I was always too inexperienced to transform
obscenity into something beautiful, but at least
you had plants like we do now, or at least

that's how my reminiscence colors your space: towering
ferns that almost looked fake, mighty tropical
leaves I didn't know the name for yet.
                              Only this,

it's silly, writing to someone I never really
cared for and hold onto through nothing
but instagram stories and suggestive leaves,
someone I wouldn't offer a slice of my life

today: you're a tired resonance and the thing is,
we are really happy, most days, and most of
the plants remind me of her, anyway—even
the comedy of human devotion can stand up

against worn longing, against the way plants,
like smell, can threaten to bring you back, the way
my mother still talks about the hard wood of her
childhood horse chestnut tree. Like wisp or tendril,

there are old, florid words that could end this poem
comely, but you're just a technicality of the past, a body
of knowledge, a proper science. So let's leave it at that:
Thaumatophyllum bipinnatifidum, even if it sounds ugly.

Shannon Pulusan

Plant Sitter

At the center of your life, you're creating forest air
in a friend's apartment. You place a ceramic bowl
beside each plant pot & pour water. Humidity,

the dewy breath of company. Of imaginary beings
sipping from the bowl little by little. You refill,
wonder where clouds form in this water cycle?

Wonder where everyone's gone to? Last night
you dreamt & remembered everything
come morning. The neighbor girl, first love,

carpool, cousins of your cousins.
You welcomed them in the basement level
of your childhood home. Blurry, how familiar you are

to people of the past. You called everyone's name
first & last, served water
by collecting the stream from a leaking pitcher.

Everything is so tedious, but you stay still
in this place that keeps you. When those you dream of
forget the skyline & the exact hours when it's blue

& blush & gray & coin   all at once,
        know home is truly   where
    every bench you sit on   faces the river   & where

a samoyed will sniff   your shoelaces. It's nice
        to be the one   to depend on
to cherish   the little reasons   & the future

        of one's roots.   You fill each bowl
            set beside each plant pot   & message your friend
    to say   everything's been   cared for.

nat raum

haworthia fasciata

my stardew valley house is full of plants
i am incapable of killing, pixelgreen luscious
leaves scattering up wooden walls
to the place where i'd put a skylight if i could
actually see the ceiling. i couldn't hope

to keep a plant alive outside pelican town—
my brain is a lemon, barely remembering to feed
itself, let alone the fifteen bundles of tangled
leaf and succulent limbs that used to live
on my windowsill in college. it's a wonder

my first zebra plant didn't shrivel sooner,
its spinywhite leaves staying plump with water
even after she once tumbled from a ceramic pot
onto the gravelgrey surface of my dormitory's
nearest parking lot. i'd named her sylvia

for no reason, and brought her along when i built
my first makeshift home in a cinderblock cube—
not long before a darkness glitched my skull
and i spent the next five years forgetting
to water the plants.

Zoe Reay-Ellers

Unread texts sent to my orchid that finally bloomed after two years while my girlfriend was taking care of it for me over the summer because I have to fly across the country to go home & she just drives

i know / i get it / she's sunlight / and nutrients / and everything / good / with hair / the color of dried-out fertilizer / and i knocked you off a windowsill / once / yes / i know / she hums / soft / under her breath / and talks sweet / to you / and i don't / have six ice cubes / like google recommends / like she pries / from freezing plastic / for you / just / water / from my bathroom sink / i'm not precise / like she is / my fingers shake / i leave the blinds / closed / or window / open / let december embed / into your aerial roots / and she's so warm / isn't she / and i only think / of myself / of coping / curled in a comforter / unmoving / except to shiver / but i scrambled / for your bark chips / when you fell / on the floor / remember / me / on my knees / apologizing / picking them / out / of / the / carpet / with my chewed nails / again / and again

arushi (aera) rege

nuclear winter, burning planet

how do you love / a forest on fire / a body on fire / wildfire / how do you love / decomposition / water under the bridge / tell me how to love / decay / how to love nature after its ruin / how to appreciate / ruin / tell me what it means to / love an invasive species / how to explain the beauty of *kudzu* / tell me how immortality is the same as *lingzhi* / how the fountain of youth / is tree rings counted / how the water of my blood / runs clear / how mango orange lights / mean that my blood stays / brown of my ancestors / tell me how to love / smoke-filled skies / bright red sunsets fade into / your lips / and i wonder how many roses i have / to buy until you understand / i'd love you past / eventual nuclear winter / fated death / fated ruin / fated love / becomes new climate crisis / becomes a burning planet / becomes a forest on fire / because wildfire becomes / decomposition / becomes loving a house on fire / tell me how immortality is / great basil brittlecone pine / forever becomes / half a second or / fourty-nine thousand years / tell me how immortality is this: / handfuls of *zoloft* shovelled into / your mouth as / you pretend you're fine / i forgot i take *prozac* / tell me how *lingzhi* is the longest living mushroom / yet it's lifespan is fourty-five / how do you love / a forest on fire / if that forest is nothing but / a body on fire / wildfire / or a hozier song / or the garden of eden / or another smiths song / & loving a house on fire / & loving salt in a wound / & loving overripe strawberries / & loving nuclear winter / fated death / fated ruin / new climate crisis becomes / a burning planet / tell me how / the water of my blood / is clear / how my blood stays the same / brown as my ancestors

heidi andrea restrepo rhodes

life cycle of ephemeral plants

Every ephemeral species has a life cycle timed
to exploit a short period when resources are freely available.

So rare it is we all get what we need. Still,
in each other's arms we briefly unfurl for spring. The rest of the year,

underground, we root & rhizome, survival strategy.
Deciduous, we shed our clothes, our skin. Petals, leaves, fruit.

Teeth come in seasons. Delicate cotton of your shirt
fluttering in drop, an abscission.

As the mariposa lilies grieve so short the seasons that favor it,
here we are in the winter of the law. An unfavorable season, deluge of delusion,

a cold of heart against our mattering. As wildflowers
lie dormant as seeds, our love sometimes waits for better weather.

All riot in the fields not without its calendars. Aster, azalea, & foxglove,
planning up ungovernable germination and splendor, an all-weather affair.

Say gay say gay say gay say gay. A proliferation. Repudiation of absence
pushing against the threshold. An invasive species, excessive in our joy.

We return though, ready to live & die & live again. Negation of negation.
The evidence of us, an echo reverberating on the skin. A fugacious record

made of woven whispers & spectacular display. An invention of hours
kissing in the dark, in the mud, in the glittering & finite minute.

Tristan Richards

Pandemic Plants & Disco Balls

Sometimes I worry that no one knows anything
about me, and then, right on the bend of my spiral,
I remember that at least five of my friends
have sent me links to the same disco ball planter.
If nothing else, at least my brand is strong.
Every sun-touched spot in my apartment glitters
with plants, and what I mean by that is I have spent
this season of loss with my eyes on growth. It started
with a snake plant and a fiddle leaf fig on my first
frantic pandemic grocery run. My friends bet against
the third plant immediately and they were correct.
Now, my favorite afternoons are the ones where I'm caught
off guard by a spray of light against my wall. It polka dots
my plants and draws my eye toward the window.
I don't have anything new to say about plants
but I want them anyway, and maybe that's the point.
Maybe all I need to do is notice that the snake plant
is still standing. Maybe today, it's okay to rest
on a simple fact and pick up the dropped leaves later.

M.P. Rosalia

sapling, taken from the northern pacific coast, kept in a jar

little tree, do you know where your roots have sprouted?
you grew so valiantly, reaching for California sun and the
branches that had made you, seeking to belong in a
copse of your brethren, but you will never belong, choked
by the mother — that is nature after all.

uprooted
by hands that have never known how to find comfort
in soil but who wanted you to live. you didn't live.
I'm sorry.

you were so young, just a little sprout, and I didn't
know how to love you. that sun you strove for choked
as much as mottled roots below the surface and,
parched, you wilted in the drought of a place where you
never had room to grow.

Margaret Saigh

THIS IS AN AUTOMATIC REPLY

I text my friend, *I'm an alienated worker in a brutal city.*

On a podcast I am told to imagine

all the roads in all the cities

filled with plants and trees and paths for people to walk.

I imagine this, and it depresses me. I used to be fascinated

by the border between the natural world

and the human one

how one world

contains one world   contains one world   contains one world —

On the way to work the bus passes several parking garages.

I try to look at the sky instead and reflect on the intimacy

of touching thighs with a stranger.

After the rain I take the collar off Zadie

and imagine the nakedness she was born into, and my own nakedness, too.

Before I merge on a highway I prepare for emotional disassembling.

I make eye contact with a robin.

I take Zadie out for a walk and the streetlight elongates our shadows on the pavement,

and there is also the moon.

When snow falls for the first time, I go to the woods and pick three aborted entoloma

which are actually two fungi, one parasitizing the other.

I cook them, pushing them around the pan gingerly with a wooden spoon

Everyone knows parasite means eating at the table of another

Jake Salazar

Red Yarrow

I stare the yarrow down—
enviously, I watch it turn the awful dirt to oxygen.
I have seen this flower grow alongside Highway 64
beneath the guard-rails, out the gravel-stones.
at home in the smog and the lead pollution.

damn that weed—
its easter-hued petals and hardy genetics;
its tolerance for the intolerable.

the garden store displays it in a section on the patio,
the "clay soil" row, with the coneflowers and rudbeckias
that happily sit in their sticky-wet soil,
their grainy silt, their muddy flower-beds.

it hurts my eyes—
their unbearable gratitude.
their Spring showing, their bold blossoms.
red yarrow, in the hostile clay, thrives.
can't I?

Nnadi Samuel

Someday, I identify as a Prairie

Glory be to the improper plot: this acre of hand tilled hibiscus
& the dying raven that slants midway, in collapsed grace.
I am thankful for everything that lays chaotic. jagged landmass.
raked mess of depression, inversely proportional to climate change—
the way I discolor in summer. measuring tape laid to waste because,
this is a farm dispute where everyone wants to outcount the other.
when Ma questions me on how I'd love to manage my existence,
I tell her *I wish to identify as a desert, barren with opportunity.*
ridges laid haphazardly—I find my loin tumbleweeding from its root.
the shower head, gone haywire. all of my dirty-washings, heaping in
the ugly fold of a mountain. It's barely summer & I have bled past two moons,
dressed my blood, midair—hacking at the tough ground that spoils into green.
hoping, my grief looks gorgeous in the face of harm. & say it doesn't, it still would
remain mine to keep. sorrow knew me in the early hours of my birth. here, look how I
wear the stench. even rain leaves petrichor as aftertaste, in the mouth of the world.
in the chewed minute, I observe night waste in plastic silence. branches shedding from
their trunk. cloth, roasting in the unforgiving heat of summer. all creature here adores
pain. It is one way to worship how we make something of it. even the blank page
adores anguish. still, I choose joy. choose to wrap my head in the moment, scream a
purple song, mow the lawn at the balcony. I joked around the blisters in my palm.
thank the edges for being jagged & improper, thank the blade's music for making a
mohawk of the grasses & the past that is a bunch of weed—ready for a haircut.
I hope to make sense of my future someday. as of now, I identify as a prairie.v

56 minutes,
including dryer cycle

doing my laundry at 3 am reminds me
of my mother clipping her plants
brown leaves sinking to the floor with
the chemical assurance of sweat stains
leaving clothes. the circular motion of
living things encapsulated in the water
cycle and washing machines
the shirt will be clean again just as
love-in-idleness will grow again,
purple potted flowers recalling
literature's purplest prose, pretentious like
nerds sitting on the field at the end of the
school day, picking blades of grass to
throw at each other, content knowing that
they won't have to get the dirt out
themselves. growing up makes me
consider everything around me in ways i
would never have thought about apart
from earth day news. such strange
emotion: looking at the rain-mulched soil,
reading about love-potion-plants, hoping
for hermia and helena to leave what has
been written and fall in love with each
other, weaving flower crowns they could

leave me the pattern to conveniently find
five centuries later for botanical attempts
at flirting. help a girl out, won't you?

Mandy Seiner

The Chernobyl Effect

Wine in Europe was never the same after the explosion,
can be dated by its radioactivity, levels of caesium-137.

The northern radiation plume swept up into Scandinavia,
the southern dusted the berry-fields of France.

It's said that you can taste the difference, can feel
the ever-nearing fallout of your own body with each sip.

American wine was sold in Sweden for the first time in 1987.
Economics is the science of unintended consequences.

The city of Pripyat is now a restored Eden,
without any god to watch over it.

The confinement zone turned refuge has saved species
from extinction, all of their skins pulsing beneath the surface.

Somewhere in Norway, someone is watching
the Northern Lights, a glass of Yakima Valley Merlot in hand.

Somewhere in Pripyat, a spider is weaving an irregular web,
a tree is growing its 39th ring,
an enormous wolf is howling its reservoir song.

Ashish Kumar Singh

Agriculture

Even before the sun climbs over our head,
granny soils her clothes by kneeling
in the tilled earth with the dedication
of a mother nursing her just-born.
She says, *it's 'birthing' what plants need,
grow, they will on their own.*
As she pats the soil over the mango kernel,
she tells me how when she was little,
she would do this all day, standing
in a field with water up to her childish
knees and push green blades of paddy
back into the earth. If she stood up
and looked around, she would see
the entire village in this same occupation,
her own mother bent in the water
with her sister strapped on her back
and father somewhere in the far distance,
his body so brown crows would mistake it
for wet mud. Later in the evening
when dinner was served, father would say,
looking at his brood of children, this.
This is happiness, just seeing you all eat.

Derek R. Smith

Poem as infiltrated tree

When there's even a chance
An alternative universe
Where we end up together,
You'll find you have become
One of those bugs that burrows pathways
In the very being of my tree.
Laborious ruts that tore away something,
Hidden just below the bark—invisible—until I'm felled.
There's no telling the damage you have done.
Moving forward as you do
Making your own trail
Perhaps contributing to
My eventual demise,
Tiny beaver gnawing at my cellulose stability.
What resilience that a forest lineage
Has been instilled in me.
My internalized tattoos force reflection
On what I have allowed
to let grow on me.
As seasons change,
The home I provide to mycelia and
Plume-ed aviators as they twitterpate,
Not to mention the rodentia I have cohabitated with.
As seasons change,
I see me change too.
My glorious autumnal fire
A dropped facade

And naked here I stand,
Then spring forth
Wearing only
My exquisite robe of rare resilience.

Sarp Sozdinler

Wetlands

we never kissed in the city
only in cattail wind
in the hush of fog-heavy reeds
where no one asked *who's who*

you called the frogs our choir
your fingers learning
what dusk does to skin

mud claimed our soles
like a second inheritance
we let it

your nail beds
smelled of algae & me

Kit Steitz

For Our Six Year Anniversary

Let's be pothos,
planted together
with deep roots in
night-dark soil,
cozy in our
terracotta,
our curling tendrils
entangled.

Two vines, in a
sunbeam; two vines
holding hands from
the deepest root
to the youngest leaf.

Liam Strong

our parents as deciduous forests of the upper midwest

blunt needles where cuffed jeans of hemlock want kindling. his mouth dead
  with kentucky

coffeetree in the plaque. we snap balsam in our pockets. you point at an elm &
  say life's a beech.

        somewhere wind stirs, somewhere

it doesn't. or the leaves stir the wind, creepers sinch around wooden ankles, &
  entrapment. even

hands as soft as northern catalpa. even stolons, the name for runners or clones

or false. even our nails, chipped & hanging on. swamp

                              white oak where she threw sheep's head

into the grist. everyone or thing standing around us is tall & holding blades.
  when black ash trees

cripple & fall,

        the process is called a failure. you can tell the run-off wants to form

a river here, or something else we don't have the veins for. we don't look at a
  samara & say

yes. that.

that will one day be what we never expected. we're told, by next solstice, the buds will

be more than veneer. we have to trust that.

Joy Su

Fertilizer

In my first home, we grew tomatoes and beanstalks
and expectations like members of the same family.
For a second, I want to be useless. I spent so much of my childhood
trying to be smart. I wanted to be a doctor, lawyer, engineer—
but mostly I just wanted to be needed. I thought myself
a gardener of sorts. Nursed people instead of plants
all the way back to life. Remember, my mother grew up on a farm.
She can't keep houseplants alive no matter how she tries.
I tried giving her light, water, air. I nearly forced her to eat.
We tended to each other like sundews unsure
what was stalk or flesh. She tells me now, *you were a good kid.*
Why get a therapist when I have you? I think of how flytraps live in bogs
but get their nitrogen from insects instead.
Remember, she grew up on a farm. Don't forget she had to leave.
I tended to my garden with fingers and pride grew up from the shoots.

Saheed Sunday

In These Ancestral Rites, We Remember our Forefathers through Strong Morsels

We know what the night is thinking. These noises of pestles
hitting mortars are loud enough to echo home. To echo all
the memories we never learnt to force down with strong
morsels of pounded yam. Mom says white is heaven.
And we have stored up enough of them in our belly
like archangels. Mom says white is divine. And we have
gulped down enough of it to make us gods. Father says
white is history. And we can see those pasts. Through
the feverish faces of the lumps of yams scattered
in our mortars like pebbles. Here, we have learnt
to never pick food that finds its way to the ground.
There are no coincidences with nature. That is the earth
working its ways to fix crumbs into the bellies of our
forefathers. Spirits whispering like good news into the ears
Of the land. Saying, here it is: here is your own portion
of these strong morsels. We tap wine like little graces into
our kegs and drink ourselves to stupor. But plantation
is trembling down its feet, and we are the fear. Its neck
droops down like a question mark, and we are the sickle.
If growth were to be a dairy product, some of us would be
lactose intolerant. We bend through harvests like acrobats
and wonder why we still fall short of belly-filled palms.

Drained feet. Hungry stomachs. How do we remember
our forefathers now if we keeping losing our strong morsels
to feeble attempts at preservation?

Luke Sutherland

Nurselog

Olympic National Park

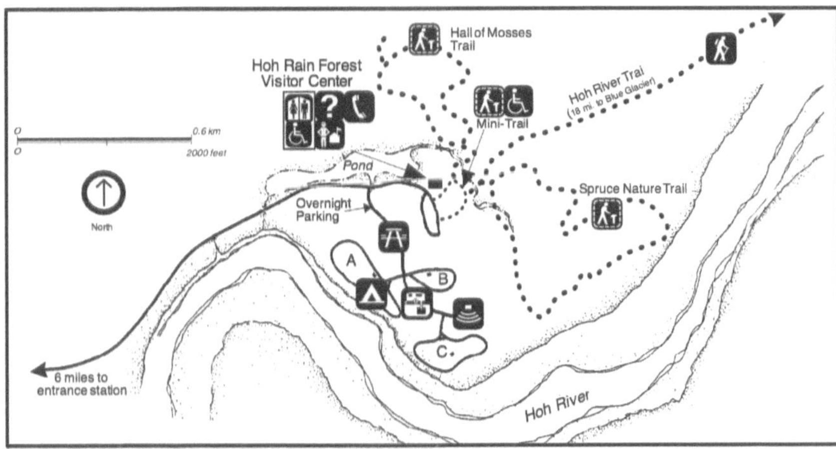

I take my shot in the Hoh Rain Forest, making sure B gets a good angle with the little disposable camera I bought at CVS. I'm always forgetting at home, letti[ng days go by before realizing I missed a dose, but here I'm buzzing for it.

My hiking bag is a temporary med kit: alcohol swabs, syringes, bandaids, two gauges of needles. I'm used to injections. Pinching the fat of my stomach, angling the needle, the one-two-three-go before the puncture. I rotate hormone days with monoclonal antibody ones. I forget about those shots, too.

The Hall of Mosses loop is short, but we spend hours on it anyway. The air is damp in my lungs, spiked with licorice fern. Lichen overwhelms the landscape. The branches of douglas-firs and Sitka spruces hang heavy under a fur of algaes. Signs along the path are lyrical and strangely charged:

[[moldering logs, trunks shaggy with moss]]
[[plant on plant]]
[[lush beards of clubmoss]]

And it's true, the lush shag of it all is romantic, bacteria and fungi fucking all around us. Lichens like leaves, like cracked paint, like gunpowder. B bends their head to inspect the composite, and their hair sheeted over their face looks like a red shrub of fruticose anchored to the bark.

I pick a spot just off the trail and lay out my supplies on a log, the glass vial of T nestled into decaying wood. I swab a spot just below my belly button while a family snakes down the path. I slide the needle into the vial and invert it, pulling thick liquid into the syringe, flicking out pockets of air. B is kneeling in the moss with the camera raised. I can hear the many small voices of the family. The point of the needle lingers over my stomach. There's murmuring, a shower of boot disturbed dirt. I try not to notice them noticing me; I've spent years practicing, but I'm not very good at it. When I finally inject, B peaks around the camera to say I look metal as hell.

The needle draws out a coin of blood as it exits my body. It sits there, tense, a blot of red amongst a stream of freckles. N, the first trans man I ever knew, taught me to hold the used syringe over my finger and squeeze the plunger one last time, swiping those precious drops across upper lip and jaw. It helps the hair grow, he said. I have no idea if this is true. I do it anyway, always, and it is the anointment that makes me whole.

The family is gone, maybe not knowing what they saw. B embraces me, and I forget it all. I love how they witness me. I love that they know which mountains are which. I love the sound they make when they are surprised. I love how they love the forest. I love that they stopped the car the moment we saw elk. I love when their head leans into my hand. I love that they refuse to eat anything I can't. For a few minutes, there is only this.

Trans Fear

When is the right time to leave? [*always*]
Is there ever a right time? [*never*]
What does that mean? [*agony*]
Where would we go? [*together*]
Who would take us? [*arms outstretched*]
Do we wait until the killings? [*it's too late*]
Do we wait until it's someone we know? [*no*]
Could we live through that vigil? [*no*]
Which of us might bury ourselves preemptively? [*yes*]
Do we count ourselves lucky? [. . .]
How could we leave, knowing who can't? [   ]

We spend a long time in the trees, on a tree, by the river. We kiss,
for lack of better answers. I use their knife to carve FAG4DYKE
into the wood. Which of us is which is a matter of opinion.

&on

Much, much later, a man — a coworker of mine, my building opposite his — will
tell the audience at a work event that trans people are pedophiles. He doesn't
say it like that exactly, but we all know what he means. I will feel rattled, sick,
jaded. I will file complaints both alone and as a group. I will despair. I will
consider quitting all of the time. I will look up the cost of my prescriptions
without insurance. Later.

Still in the forest, B and I stand in front of a plaque telling us that we are looking
at a nurselog. The massive trunk lays prone on the floor. Nooks of its body collect
detritus. Moss, needles, leaf litter and squirrel shit — a mattress of lush humus
for sprouting seedlings. A colonnade of mature hemlocks straddle the log from
which they grew. In another spot, the nurselog has rotted away completely.
Nutrients cycle, burls break down. Its children stand on tented roots, hollow
air where their parent used to be, not able to let go of the shape.

A nurselog is like a whale fall. A nurselog is like a transsexual living past their life expectancy.

Have I ever told N that he made my life possible? That I'm still on stilts, alive over the space he made?

Dihya Tamaghza

Watching the Springtime Blooms Instead of the News

An intoxicating fragrance of blue hyacinth
pulls a gentle blanket of tranquillity over
forlorn eyes. Warming spring sun lulls us
into a foolish haze. Cross keyed primroses
in Druidic robes of hopeful yellow guard
the pearly gates of heaven. On the threshold,
spy the wallflower sentinels standing tall
warding off evil like a Mediterranean eye.
Marsh-bound iris holds sure, steadfast with
a relentless hope no slick mud could diffuse.
Shoots spring forth from crimsoned ground.
See white daffodils mourning, wide-eyed,
heralding death in numb prayer over graves
of massacred peoples, watchful and judging.
Slender foxglove holds immortality in its cups,
leaves spear-like in a tense bravery manifest.
Martyrs drink their fill of her bounty and ascend.
Transformative lungwort awakens travellers
into fresh renewal, promising a life eternal.
Witness the gentil nature of lily-of-the-valley
ushering in new beginnings, a novel shot at
mythical happiness. At the end of the Garden,
a lone white poppy bobs its solemn head,
nodding off to sleep.

Addie Tsai

SWOONING FOR SUCCULENTS

The first time I fell in love with a succulent was the first time I fell in love with
a woman. She had a mess of bright orange curls the same shade as my favorite
summertime drink. By the time she introduced me to succulents we were no
longer in love, but in complicated friendship. I'd like to think that I was her
most prized subject, even though I'm well aware that this was what led to our
dissolution. Either she or another woman she loved to capture, a well-known
belly dancer, in the round black lens, her magnified eye, gained temporary
access to a house that belonged to the rich. I couldn't for the life of me tell you
what they did to acquire such treasures, but I remembered that the house they
owned had a magnificent pool surrounded by succulent gardens framed with
wood. The red-headed girl took photos of the belly dancer and me, separate,
and also together, nude except for the sweat that dripped down our pale skin,
the sun determined to redden it by the day's end. I couldn't tell you what it was
that drew me to the succulents' bulbous leaves that looked animated, or at the
very least, edible, soft yet durable. When I proposed to a man a few years later,
I spent hours scouring the internet for succulent bouquets — I was thrilled there
was such a thing! — but ultimately ended up going with a small bouquet hand-
picked at a farm a drive's distance from where we wed, and more affordable. My
mother had always had what she called a "purple thumb," killing every growing
thing in her path. She was prone to believe that every tragedy that befell her was
genetic, and so even as my father's green thumb transformed our backyard into
a tropical paradise, I never did buy plants, except for a grocery store orchid or
two. But then, when my marriage wilted slowly, and all at once, and COVID
kept lives out when I most needed them to be in, I drove myself to my favorite

nursery and bought the succulent that asked for me to come closer. A friend offered me a cactus plant, and a couple of other succulents, but it was this one that decided to thrive, alongside me, slowly, steadily, like all of us.

Ann Tweedy

inner limits

dad, my love for you could be
a potted orchid: chipped bark,
climate control, delicate
watering preferences. like other
growers, i'd order my life
around rare, uncertain

flowerings. or is it
better anchored in a terra cotta
pot emitting more sturdy
greenery? silver inch or spider
plant or something tropical whose name
will never stick on my tongue—
even a cactus in coarse desert soil,
unable to bear abundance.

Arya Vishin

LAST WINTER YOU LEAVE ME UNPLANTED

& when you come back I will garland,
I will wreath, I will carnation, I will
braid gendhekaphool thick & globular,
I will inflorescence, I will faith, I will
doveaglecrow, my mouth will form the
words you tell me, I will blossom crêpe
paper jasmine delicate & jagged, you
will flush greater flamingo whitepink,
we will unearth with our pinnate hands
letting the soil imbibe & absorb into
frondfingers, I will not bury something,
I will not bury something, & I will not
bury something.

Nikki Wallschlaeger

Mother of Thousands

"Bryophyllum daigremontianum, commonly called devil's backbone, mother-of-millions, mother-of-thousands, alligator plant, or Mexican hat plant is a succulent plant native to Madagascar."

Underneath the fields is where our stories are buried. The monocrops were decisions made about our past, so I ask you to take the batteries out of the clanging wall clock before I go to sleep to prevent the supremacist art of domestication from permeating my dreams.

Inside of my raised fist is a struggling livelihood: there is sugar cane, corn, and certainly cotton. I've come here to climb the spiral rope back to the knowledge of the land, holding a scythe branded with the name i gave myself & my hands ache so much from having to dig you out,

I stop at every county cemetery no matter who is resting there. I am a gatherer of thousands, how you said we don't have to buy seeds driving past a town named Coon Valley as I inwardly flinch about a strange joke E. used to make about not seeing a relative "in a coon's age,"

and the day i realized what she meant by that when she said it, how my fist in the will of my stomach began to wilt, all their freshly mowed lawns burning with the crosses of their wickedness. a mother ushering her children to safety a story carried on by the next generation of plantlets,

since water has been proven to secure history, when public wailing feels like you're a conduit for someone else. Caring for an unmarked grave on her lunch hour, autocratic fields you can see from an airline window seat. We touch our callused feet together. Underneath this land is a succulent downpour we are building from the lives calling to be excavated. The fists of black & brown women throughout the ages in a controlled heirloom heat. Seeds taking flight from the ancient fields of our wildflower palms for we are the mothers of thousands

Sasha Weiss

remember

that time i threw up on you outside the ketamine clinic
and we lay facedown on your apartment floor
smelling the carpet and talking about camping trips
we have never been camping together
but i love biting you in the forest til your knees give out
and your thigh highs are covered in pine needles

Keagan Wheat

Our Breakup Plant

You picked a name
without a square of sunlight
for a fucking succulent.

Your mezzanine superiority
left my gift for dead.
Maybe gleaming eyes &

upturned voice aren't
as honest as I believe.
Maybe these eyes mark

something as real as
reflection. Your
saucer eyes plate

for bake off, not
the substance behind
a potluck.

Cassandra Whitaker

It's Not Who You Are But Where You Are

A sycamore dominates Its limbs crown   the canopy—it's hard straight
top—its trunk
thick and round as three barrels The forest   slopes south—and south the
forest slides
into pine—but here sycamores hold the forest   with its champion thickness—
the thickness
furrowed with a mind that wishes for swifts   —wishes for time to spread nutlets
across earth—
soft and dark—pioneering—following the sun—   west as west can grow—leave the
rest behind
A tree moves one sapling at a time—the forest   scurrying along by the
roots—the young
sycamore just a bit further west toward the sun—   the pioneer sycamore—whose
top crowns
the forest canopy before the forest slopes south   into pine—but here sycamores
hold the forest
with its champion thickness furrowed with a mind   for swifts that no longer come
and wishes
to leave behind the pines—the old forest   thinning or thickening or
rotting with vine
and undergrowth—westward seeking—seeking   clarity—seeking the end of
the question—bending like a bridge—ever asking—never answered

Elizabeth Wing

Entanglement

Over the barbed wire, under the sweet thorniness of it, around the rootbulb,
strangling the dog rose. Between clematis and snowberry. Twisted with fennel
and tree of heaven.   Blooming into morning glory, into knotweed.
Weaving our fingers through our tangled hair. Pulling kinked strands for the
nesting birds.

Blooming back into the summer spent hacking back blackberries. As we grew
into machete-swingers, sunkissed, strong. Twisted into vines tough as rope,
grooved deep fiber   meshed in with thorns big as cat claws.

Under the best of intentions. Growing into the spiked alien-green head
of the mock cucumber, blooming into a fuckage of snails. Blooming into
the listening well. Blooming into the flank of the culvert. Blooming into
luminous distraction. Inextricable from a boy who rappelled out of a locked
quarantine third story balcony with a piece of hemp rope to come eat
tangerines with you.

Held in a dying grapevine, bloomed with yeast. Inextricable from a boy who
said he could make water into wine give him grapes and six weeks. Who said
he would weave a crown of thorns and wear it if you told him to. Our arms
cross hatched with scratches for trying

Over hedgerows, under property lines, around distinction. Between profit
margins. Tightening in this unseasonable heat, choked by its own green
hunger. Choked by the attempted depiction. Blooming into the purple
thrum of nightshade, fruiting into the promise of trouble.   Twisted in the
bottom of the milk jug.

Inextricable from the girl who stabbed me in the knee with a plastic fork after
I shaved her head, in the chaos of snow geese lifting off the field, meshed in
our hands. Held in everything I've bought and broken. Sheltered by our own
deadwood, sheltered by our own dry brush where rattlesnakes laze.

Under the foundation, around the median, where a feral cat hides her kittens
in the oleander. Weaved back to bloom into every kitchen slow dance.
Meshed in fishing wire and horsehair,   dental floss and string. Place
held in the chaos of memory, sheltered by obscurity. The rabbit tunneling
through the brush. Someday I will wrestle this into song

Anangookwe Wolf

i want clean water god dammit

when was the last time–I saw a firefly humming their love poem, weaving
through blueberry brush

when was the last time–I woke to a cacophony of: twiney chickadees, jovial
robins, mocking blue jays, the chattering loon, or a ravens throaty call cutting
through morning dew

leaded smog in place of hazy fog–dimming mornings light

deafening screams from the R46–piss and shit (is it human or dog) overwhelm
the senses, my eyes burn   *I long for the home that was swept
away by murky waters*

when was the last time–I swam downstream with the bluegills, sifting through
algae coated rocks for crawfish and clams as my nephew laughed and screamed
in the sandbar

when was the last time   *when did it*   happen

it was gradual   *ignored* happen(ed)

it started with the fish, washed ashore, coated in iridescence
then came   hushed evergreen sprigs rattled only by wind, ardent calls absent
within boreal

songs of solace overrode by dozers   a deafening silence is sweeping
the land

i don't want concrete   I want clean water

Julia Yong

a step to heaven and/or

a garden yet to be planted:
what if the both of us, yet
to be planted in the dearth
of two simple suns, amber
       undoing winter's wrongs.
a tie around her pinky finger
       reminds that flesh is fleeting
       similar to a kitchen glow,
       echoing across this apartment
       that is altogether ours echo
       echo the same song needs
       to, need to play an oblivion
         of spells when the rain forgets
you're wondering when the
       poem gets green, when the
       ikea table is unearthed from
       paint chips and is cast out
       the bay window an all-out
       tantrum where belongings
       revolt and build communes
         from every one avocado pit
the queen swallowtail sits at
       her new desk, awaiting every
       other surface that supervenes
       for an entire little life, brims
       with infinite cinnamon scrolls
       and folds into a two month

yoga stint, no one ever told me
that a habit could make you
            believe in new things again
words mince garlic buds
        (a seed drops in the space
        between them and now)
        something mornings dipped
        dewey drooling a mouth open
        the day perching beside us
            asking what's for breakfast

Allya Yourish

The corn sweats

it's why the summers
in Iowa
are so humid

Actually it draws water
up from the earth
passing wetness
weighing down
open air

I was drawn up
from the earth
but swamp (I wish
I didn't have to claim
that) not prairie

Untouched prairie is
unfathomably rare
so much stripped
turned farm turned
CAFO

The stench of a CAFO
is also unfathomable
as in beyond imagining
death on the nose

But beyond the corn
and the pigs
is a swimming hole

Horses are there too

And it is 92 degrees
and Iowa humid
and I am laying
on a blanket
with this poem

Iowa also has a lot
of poems but maybe that's
just my Iowa
my private collision
with land and sky

There is so much sky here
it unfurls in every direction
begging poetry

Everyone I know
has written a poem
on the sky

Today my poem
sits under
vast blue
and those white wispy
clouds that beg
for oil paint

Today we are swimming

And that big sky hangs
overhead air gold and thick
with early summer

And my poem calls across
murky cool water
calls to every Iowa poem Iowa
sky Iowa summer
with corn-heavy wind

Contributors

Rasha Abdulhadi is calling on you—yes you, even as you read this—to renew your commitment to refusing and resisting genocide of the Palestinian people. May your commitment to Palestinian liberation deepen your commitment to your own. May your exhaustion deepen your resolve and make you immovable. May we all be drawn irresistibly closer to refusals that are as spectacular as the violence waged against our peoples.

March Abuyuan-Llanes is a writer and poet from Quezon City, Philippines. They have work in *This Is Southeast Asia*, *Ghost City Review*, *Haluhalo Journal*, and elsewhere. They are the editor of *LIGÁW*, an anthology zine of militant poetry from emerging LGBTQ+ Filipino writers, and are a founding member of Kinaiya: Kolektib ng mga LGBTQIA++ na Manunulat. Besides writing, they are a peasant advocate of Artista ng Rebolusyong Pangkultura (ARPAK).

Saida Agostini is a queer Afro-Guyanese poet whose work explores how Black folks harness mythology to enter the fantastic. Her work is featured or forthcoming in *Diode*, The Academy of American Poets' *Poem-a-Day*, *Poet Lore*, *Plume*, amongst others. Saida's work can be found in several anthologies, including *Not Without Our Laughter: Poems of Humor, Sexuality and Joy*. Her full length collection *let the dead in* was released by Alan Squire Publishing (March 2022). A Cave Canem Graduate Fellow, Saida is a Best of the Net Finalist.

Ashia Ajani is a sun shower, an overripe nectarine, a carnivorous plant, a glass bead. They are the author of one poetry collection, *Heirloom* (Write Bloody Publishing, 2023) and a forthcoming collection of lyric essays, *Tending the Vines* (Timber Press). Her writing is a kaleidoscope of her work as an eco-griot & abolitionist.

Mair Allen is a writer living in Minneapolis, MN. A current MFA candidate at Antioch University, their work can be found in *Hooligan Mag's Spilled Ink feature*, *Griffel*, *Kithe*, *Oroboro*, and *Aurora*. They were the 2020 Mikrokosmos Poetry Prize winner, and placed second in the 2021 Penrose Poetry Prize. Their prized plant is a vanilla orchid that just sent out a second vine. When not writing they can be found.

Ally Ang is a gaysian poet based in the occupied Duwamish and Coast Salish lands known as Seattle. Ally is a Jack Straw Writers Program fellow and an editor for Game Over Books and Floating Bridge Press. Their work has been published in *Muzzle Magazine*, *Foglifter*, *The Journal*, and elsewhere.

Crisosto Apache is from Mescalero, New Mexico, on the Mescalero Apache reservation. Crisosto is Mescalero Apache, Chiricahua Apache, and Diné (Navajo) of the Salt Clan, born for the Towering House Clan. Institute of American Indian Arts, MFA alumni, and a professor of English. Crisosto is also an editor-at-large for *The Offing*. Apache's books are *GENESIS* (Lost Alphabet) & *Ghostword* (Gnashing Teeth Publishing), winner of the Publishing Triangle's 2023 Betty Berzon Emerging Writers Award and a finalist for the 2023 Colorado Authors League Award in poetry. His poetry collection *is(ness)* is available from Gnashing Teeth Publishing. Apache is also a two-time Pushcart Prize nominee.

Robin Arble (she/her) is from western Massachusetts. Her poems have appeared in *2River*, *ALOCASIA*, *beestung*, *Impossible Task*, *Midway Journal*, *Poetry Online*, *Passages North*, *the tiny*, and *Up The Staircase Quarterly*, among others. Raised in Holyoke, she studied comparative literature and creative writing at Hampshire College and lives in New York.

sterling-elizabeth arcadia is a Best of the Net winning and Pushcart Prize nominated trans poet and lover of birds, cats, and her friends, living in philadelphia. Their work has been published in venues including *HAD*, *ANMLY*, *beestung*, *New Delta Review*, and *Poetry Online*. Her debut chapbook, *Heaven, Ekphrasis*, is out now from Kith Books.

Guérin Asante (any/all) is a Black, queer post-disciplinary artist and plantsperson who, when not creating, belongs to four gardens and six trees.

lae astra (they/them) is an agender trans artist and writer who calls Tokyo home. Their writing has appeared in *Astrolabe, Gone Lawn, Overheard, Star*Line, Strange Horizons,* and elsewhere. They are a Pushcart, Best Microfiction, and Rhysling Award nominee.

Bryce Baron-Sips is an ex-biologist, current perfume collector, and insufferable opera buff living in Uppsala, Sweden. If his writing is not over the top, he has probably been replaced by a robot. His work has been published in *The Woodward Review, Revolute, Strange Horizons,* and elsewhere.

June Beck is a Diné writer from Arizona. He dabbles in photography, cross-disciplinary storytelling, and comedy. His work has previously appeared in *The Adroit Journal.*

Elizabeth Hart Bergstrom is a queer, chronically ill writer whose work appears or is forthcoming in *Bennington Review, Michigan Quarterly Review, New Orleans Review, Passages North, Uncanny,* and elsewhere. They were born in the foothills of the Blue Ridge Mountains of Virginia on Monacan land.

Jacob J Billingsley is a queer guy who blushes at the word "man." His work has appeared in *ALOCASIA, ANMLY, Empty Room Radio*'s "compulsion petal," on social media, and in his DMs. His sibling gave him a now-giant Cereus as a housewarming gift, and his backyard has more *Ageratina* in it every year. He can kind of drive.

Yasmine Bolden (they/them) is a Black American 22-year-old poet, teacher, and playwright who adores the moon from unceded Susquehannock land. They've been nominated for a Pushcart Prize, Best of the Net, and American Voices designation, and their poems have been planted in *the lickity~split,* The Feminist Center for Creative Work, and *Rootwork Journal,* among other magical locales. They attend Johns Hopkins University as a Writing Seminars and Africana Studies double major. Whatever you do, don't ask them about queering August Wilson's *Gem of the Ocean* (they'll talk until you're ready to visit the City of Bones yourself).

Joefel Bolo is a queer writer from the Philippines. Their work has appeared or is forthcoming in *The Harvard Advocate*, *fifth wheel press*, *beestung*, and elsewhere.

Slater By The Sea no longer exists.

Caroliena Cabada writes fiction and poetry. Her work has been published in *Hawai'i Pacific Review*, *Elysium Review*, *ONE ART*, and elsewhere. Her first book of poetry, *True Stories*, is available from Unsolicited Press.

Jody Chan is a writer, drummer, organizer, and therapist based in Toronto/Tkaronto. They are the author of *haunt* (Damaged Goods Press), *all our futures* (PANK), and *sick* (Black Lawrence Press), winner of the 2018 St. Lawrence Book Award, and 2021 Trillium Award for Poetry. They are also a performing member with RAW Taiko Drummers.

Maya Cheav is an environmental justice organizer and writer. Her writing has been featured or forthcoming in *Bizarrchitecture Magazine*, *Scapegoat Review*, and *Stone of Madness Press*. Cheav's debut poetry chapbook, *Lykaia*, was published with Bottlecap Press in February 2023. She is a Tin House 2024 Winter Online Workshop member and Best Small Fictions nominee. She can often be found talking to sidhe fae at the Lake of Avalon.

Grant Chemidlin is a queer poet and currently, an MFA candidate at Antioch University-Los Angeles. He is the author of the chapbook *New in Town* (Bottlecap Press, 2022) and the illustrated collection *He Felt Unwell (So He Wrote This)*. His second collection of poems *What We Lost in the Swamp* was published by Central Avenue Publishing in 2023. He's been a finalist for the Gival Press Oscar Wilde Award, the Philip Levine Prize for Poetry, and *Atlanta Review's* International Poetry Contest. Recent work has appeared or is forthcoming in *Quarterly West*, *Iron Horse Literary Review*, *Tupelo Quarterly*, and *Atlanta Review*, among others. "Cruising" appears in the recent book, *In the Middle of a Better World*, published by Central Avenue Poetry, 2026.

Chloe Chou is a freshman at Stanford University. She has served as the California State Youth Poet Laureate and the founder and the editor-in-chief of

Cloudy Magazine. Her work and writing has been recognized by the US House of Representatives, CA State Senate and Legislature, Bennington Young Writers Awards, Scholastic Art & Writing, JUST POETRY!!!, and more.

Kai Coggin (she/her) is the inaugural Poet Laureate of the City of Hot Springs, and author of five collections, most recently *Mother of Other Kingdoms* (Harbor Editions, 2024) and *Mining for Stardust* (FlowerSong Press, 2021). She is a Certified Master Naturalist, a K-12 Teaching Artist in poetry with the Arkansas Arts Council, a CATALYZE grant fellow from the Mid-America Arts Alliance, and host of the longest running consecutive weekly open mic series in the country—Wednesday Night Poetry.

Seth Copeland's work has appeared in *Puerto del Sol, The Shore, Seneca Review, Poet Lore,* and *Painted Bride Quarterly,* among others. Since 2016, he has edited *petrichor,* a digital archive of text and image. He is a lecturer at the University of Wisconsin-Whitewater and co-host of the Tabi Po reading series and open mic in Milwaukee.

Chiara Di Lello is a queer writer and educator. She loves coffee, art, and bees, and unequivocally supports the movement for Palestinian liberation. Her debut chapbook, *CHILDLESS MILLENNIAL,* was published by Game Over Books in 2026. Born and raised in New York City, she now resides in the so-called Hudson Valley.

Sara Eddy's second full-length poetry collection, *How to Wash a Rabbit,* is forthcoming from Cornerstone Press. She is also author of *Ordinary Fissures* (2024), and two chapbooks: *Full Mouth* (2020) and *Tell the Bees* (2019). Her poems have appeared in many online and print journals, including *Threepenny Review, Raleigh Review, Sky Island,* and *Baltimore Review,* among others. Her poems have been nominated for Pushcart and Best of Net Prizes, and she was the recipient of Causeway Literature's poetry award. She lives in Amherst, Massachusetts, in a house built by Emily Dickinson's cousin.

Ena Elder-Gomes (she/her) is a queer, Indigenous mother from the Yanomami nation, currently living on Wolastoqiyik land. Ena's work is rooted in a deep love for the natural world and guided by the teachings of Pacha Mama (Mother Earth). She has performed spoken word poetry at community open mics and has been published in *CUUWA Magazine*.

Emdash AKA Emily Lu Gao (高璐璐) says FREE PALESTINE and FUCK ICE. They are a poet, artist, and daughter of Chinese immigrants. She writes to heal, grow, and decolonize. Until January 2026, her poem installation *Letter B* was on view at The Chinese American Museum of Los Angeles as part of the *(Be)Spoken Poetry* exhibit. She believes in poetry's power to buoy humanity and build community. For two years she produced, hosted, and curated The Word Bookstore Open Mic in Jersey City, NJ. Along with being a Lambda Fellow, They've received funding from Sundress Publications, Bread Loaf Environmental Writers Conference, Jersey City Arts Council, and more. She has an BA in Asian American Studies from Pitzer College and an MFA in Creative Writing from Rutgers University-Newark. They are Missouri-born, Southern California-raised, and based in anxiety.

Danielle Shandiin Emerson is a Diné writer from Shiprock, New Mexico on the Navajo Nation. Her clans are Tłaashchi'i (Red Cheek People Clan), born for Ta'neezaahnii (Tangled People Clan). Her maternal grandfather is Ashííhí (Salt People Clan) and her paternal grandfather is Táchii'nii (Red Running into the Water People Clan). She has a BA in Education Studies and a BA in Literary Arts from Brown University. She has received fellowships from GrubStreet, Lambda Literary, The Diné Artisan + Author Capacity Building Institute, Ucross Foundation, Vermont Studio Center, Tin House, The Highlight Foundation, and Monson Arts. She has work published in *swamp pink, Poets.org, Yellow Medicine Review, Poetry Magazine, Thin Air Magazine, The Chapter House Journal, Poetry Northwest,* and others. Her writing centers healing, kinship, language-learning, and Diné narratives. She is an incoming MFA Fiction graduate student at Vanderbilt University.

Cherolyn Kay Fischer is a second-generation water protector, parent, and musician who learned poetry from her mother. She writes to mend relationships with nature, honor ancestors, and make sense of the upside-down world we live in. Cherolyn has Anishinaabe and European heritage and lives in Mni Sóta Makoce / Minneapolis, MN.

Aerik Francis is a Queer Black & Latinx poet and teaching artist based in Denver, Colorado, USA. Aerik is the author of the poetry chapbooks *BODYELECTRONIC* (Trouble Department, 2022) and *MISEDUCATION* (NDR, 2023).

Ryan Tito Gapelu is a Sāmaoan poet and English teacher specializing in contemporary Pasifika poetry, literature, and creative writing. His work blends traditional Sāmaoan and Pasifika themes with western literary forms, exploring identity, storytelling, and decolonized poetics.

Moni Garcia (they/them) is a queer Latine artist and poet from Illinois. They received their MFA from Arizona State University, and have been published or forthcoming in *Foglifter Journal, NOTHING HERE IS CORRECT AND IT IS DELICIOUS: a zine dedicated to the CW, Voicemail Poems,* and elsewhere.

Francis Gene-Rowe works with poetry, games, and science fiction, and teaches media practices at the University of Southampton. As well as *ALOCASIA,* you can find their poetry in *Strange Realism (Future Natures)* and *Corroding the Now: Poetry and Science|SF* (Veers Books & Crater Press). Francis is a co-director of the London Science Fiction Research Community, and has published critical work on petrocultures, cyberpunk, Ursula K. Le Guin, and Philip K. Dick. At present, Francis is hoping to think, learn, and create around speculative divination, losing in games, and goblin futures.

June Gervais's illustrated novel *Jobs for Girls with Artistic Flair* (Penguin Books/Penguin Random House Audio) is the coming-of-age story of a young queer woman becoming a tattoo artist in the 1980s. It has been featured in Lambda Literary's "Most Anticipated LGBTQIA+ Literature," *Autostraddle*'s "Rainbow Reading," *Shondaland*'s "Pride Month Reading List," and more. June's poems, essays, and stories have appeared in *Literary Hub, Writers Digest, RHINO, North American Review, Them, Sojourners, Bennington Review, Big Fiction, The Common, Cordella,* and elsewhere. She holds an MFA from the Bennington Writing Seminars.

Paul Goudarzi-Fry is a gay poet and amateur photographer from central New Hampshire. He is a graduate of the Rainier Writing Workshop at PLU, and his poems have appeared in *Travesties?!* and *DarkWinter Lit.* His favorite plant is *Lavandula angustifolia.*

Rhienna Renée Guedry (they/she) is a writer and interdisciplinary artist based in Portland, Oregon from the Gulf Coast. A 2024 Lambda Fellow, three-time Pushcart Prize nominee, and 2022 Tin House Workshop alum, you can find their work in *Maudlin House, Southern Humanities Review, Bayou Magazine, Muzzle,* and elsewhere.

Jo Güstin is a multilingual writer and producer who uses fiction, comedy, poetry, and philosophy to understand and enjoy both herself and the world. In 2020, she launched the award-winning production company Dearnge Society to champion intersectional social justice through stories that make you laugh, dream, and reflect. One day, when she grows up, she'll write BL smut—right now, she's just too scared.

annakai hayakawa geshlider's work has been published in *Hanging Loose Magazine, Actually People,* and *Rad Families: A Celebration.* her chapbook, *newname road,* was published by Kaya Press in March 2025. she lives near the mother ditch of a river.

narinda heng is a queer, Khmer American writer, climber, and potter living on Ohlone land. Her work centers the complexities of history, place, and identity.

Marcy Rae Henry is a multidisciplinary Xicana artist from the Borderlands who loves succulents, purple tulips, and red roses. She is the author of *death is a mariachi* (Bauhan Press), which was winner of the May Sarton NH Poetry Prize, *when to go to the Taj Mahal* (Bottlecap Press), *the body is where it all begins* (Querencia Press), *dream life of night owls* (Open Country Press), which was winner of the Open Country Chapbook Contest, and *We Are Primary Colors* (DoubleCross Press) . Her work has received a Chicago Community Arts Assistance Grant, an Illinois Arts Council Fellowship, a Pushcart nomination, and first prize in Suburbia's Novel Excerpt Contest. MRae is a professor of English, Literature and Reading, and creative writing at Wilbur Wright College, a Hispanic-Serving Institution, and an associate editor for *RHINO*. She is a digital minimalist with no social media accounts.

KateLynn Hibbard's books are *Sleeping Upside Down*, *Sweet Weight*, and *Simples*, winner of the 2018 Howling Bird Press Poetry Prize. Some journals where her poems have appeared include *Barrow Street*, *Ars Medica*, *Nimrod*, and *Prairie Schooner*. Editor of *When We Become Weavers: Queer Female Poets on the Midwest Experience*, she teaches at Minneapolis College, sings with One Voice Mixed Chorus, and lives with many pets and her spouse Jan, in Saint Paul, Minnesota. "Unblossoming" is the title poem from her new book, which is now available from Tiger Bark Press.

Nora Hikari (she/her) is an Asian American transgender poet and artist based in Philadelphia. She was a 2022 Lambda Literary fellow, and her work is published or forthcoming in *Ploughshares*, *Washington Square Review*, *Palette Poetry*, *Foglifter*, *The Journal*, and others. Her chapbook, *GIRL* 2.0 (Seven Kitchens Press, 2022) was a Robin Becker Series winner. She is a reader at the 2022 Dodge Poetry Festival and a finalist for the Red Hen Press Benjamin Saltman Award.

Ellie Howard is a trans-nonbinary poet from Georgia. They were previously published in *the Eclectic*, *Lammergeier*, and *beestung*, and are a 2022 Rhysling Award finalist. Their chapbook, *Blood Loom*, is out with Bottlecap Press. In their spare time, Ellie is learning to mimic the different bird calls heard around their apartment complex.

Talicha J. is a Black queer poet, teaching artist, and Pushcart Prize nominee. She curates workshops and virtual writing retreats that foster growth and connection. Her work appears in several literary journals, and her chapbook, *Taking Back the Body*, was released in 2024.

Umang Kalra is a writer from India and the founding EIC of *VIBE*. Their work has appeared or is forthcoming in *Strange Horizons*, *Wax Nine*, *Lucy Writers Platform*, and elsewhere. They are a two-time Best of the Net Anthology finalist and a Pushcart nominee.

Esmé Kaplan-Kinsey is a California transplant studying creative writing in Portland, Oregon. In their work, they are interested in exploring human-nature relation and deconstructing binaries that cast humankind in opposition to the natural world. Their writing appears or is forthcoming in publications such as *The Adroit Journal, SmokeLong Quarterly, JMWW,* and *Gone Lawn.* They are a prose reader for *VERDANT,* a mediocre guitarist, an awe-inspiring procrastinator, and a truly terrible swimmer.

Mukethe Kawinzi lives and works on a ranch in california. she loves the goats and adores the grass but is happy, in recent months, to be in the world alongside humans once more.

Seren Kilig (any/siya) is a Tibatib plant. Native to the Philippines, they have been replanted in North American soil, where they continue to create art. As with any uprooted, Earth-loving specimen, they call for the liberation of Palestine, Sudan, and those who continue to suffer from the toxins of imperialism, colonialism, and genocide. They encourage you to do the same. Seren has received writing fellowships from Periplus, Lambda Literary, and Roots. Wounds. Words., (among others). In their free time, they attempt challenge runs of video games. Collect mushrooms with them.

Rebecca Kinkade-Black is a Diné amateur poet. When she's not writing or tending to her plants, she likes to spend time with her wife, her parents, and their dog.

Tara Labovich (they/them, MFA) is a writer and lecturer of English and Creative Writing in Iowa. Their multi-genre creative work explores questions of queerness, survivorship, and multicultural upbringing. Their writing is nominated for Best of the Net, and can be found in journals such as *Salt Hill* and *The Citron Review.*

BEE LB is an array of letters, bound to impulse; a writer creating delicate connections. they have called any number of places home; currently, a single yellow wall on unceded Anishinaabe land in Michigan. they have been published in *Revolute Lit, After the Pause,* and *Roanoke Review,* among others. they are the 2022 winner of the Bea Gonzalez Prize for Poetry.

Jessica Le is the author of the chapbook *The Nearest Sweetest Thing* (Anstruther Press, 2021). Her work has been published in *Watch Your Head: Writers & Artists*

Respond to the Climate Crisis (Coach House Books, 2020), *The Rumpus, Salt Hill Journal, PRISM International,* and elsewhere. She lives in Toronto.

Nolan Lee is a poet and short story writer from New Jersey who wishes he wasn't from New Jersey. He has previously been published in *Elán, Vext,* and *indicia.*

j marvain is a transfem creative from delaware. she believes all mammals are just different shapes of rat, and all emotions are in tune with shifts in nature. to her, there is no greater love than community and solidarity.

celina mcmanus (they/she) is a poet, educator, youth worker, and gardener from the foothills of the Smoky Mountains, territory of the Cherokee, now living in St. Paul, MN, Dakota and Anishinaabe land. They were of the first cohort to graduate from the Randolph MFA program where they were a poetry editor for *Revolute.* Their work has been featured in *Hooligan Magazine, Peach Mag,* and others. They spend their free time tinkering at their work-in-progress, in abolitionist work, and by and in bodies of water. At the woven rush intersection of their day-to-day, they reflect on adrienne maree brown's observation that "all organizing is science fiction."

Rita Mookerjee is Assistant Professor of Interdisciplinary Studies at Worcester State University. She is the author of *False Offering* (JackLeg Press, 2023). Her poems can be found in *The Baltimore Review, New Orleans Review, The Offing, Poet Lore,* and *Vassar Review.* She serves as an editor at *Split Lip Magazine,* Sundress Publications, and *Honey Literary.*

Tiffany Morris is an L'nu'skw (Mi'kmaw) bi cis anarchafeminist writer from Mi'kma'ki. She is the author of the ecohorror novella *Green Fuse Burning* and the Elgin Award-winning horror poetry collection *Elegies of Rotting Stars.*

Sreeja Naskar is a young poet based in India. Her work has appeared in *Poems India, Crowstep Journal,* ONE ART, *Ink Sweat & Tears, FRiGG, The Chakkar, Trace Fossils Review,* and elsewhere. When she isn't writing, she's watching sad films, talking to her houseplants, or overanalyzing Bon Iver lyrics.

Miriam Navarro Prieto (she/her), Spanish artist drifting from performance to visual arts, currently focused on life-drawing the most-diverse-possible humans, and writing poems on autobiography, ecology, gender, queerness, and the politics of memory. Her first self-published poem collection *Todo está vivo* is also available online in English as *Everything Is Alive*, translated by the author. Her poems have been featured in *The Pinch* and *Paranoid Tree*, among other journals, and her illustrations in *The Winnow*. *Ecognosis*, her second poetry collection in Spanish, was a finalist for the I Premio de Poesía Letraversal (Letraversal Publishing House's I Poetry Contest), and refuses to be put in a drawer; it will come out someday, somehow. For the last three years, she's been sending out a monthly bilingual newsletter-podcast on her creative process, with plant trivia, and translated literature. Right this moment she's anxiously waiting for an acceptance for her first poetry chapbook in English, a reflection on her Post-Spanish-Civil-War ancestry.

Sarah "Nnenna Loveth" Umelo Uzoma Nwafor (they/she) is an Igbo lesbian poet, performer, and facilitator. Their work explores Black g*rlhood, Black queerness, Igbo Cosmology, sensual play, and rituals of healing. Nnenna published their chapbook, *Already Knew You Were Coming*, with Game Over Books in January of 2022, and a full-length self-published collection of poetry, *Situationship Bingo* in 2025. Nnenna has also been featured on *Button Poetry*, WBUR's *The ARTery*, *VIBEs Magazine*, Ujima *Wire*, and elsewhere. When Nnenna is not writing, they are somewhere being romanced by the intensity of life. When they speak, their ancestors are pleased.

AJ O'Reilly (they/them) is a nonbinary writer, performer, and walk-taker living in Portland, OR. Recently nominated for Best of the Net, their recent short nonfiction appears or is forthcoming in *SmokeLong Quarterly*, *HAD*, *ALOCASIA*, *Door Is A Jar*, and *Six Sentences*. Right now — like really right now, no matter what time it is where you are reading this — they are listening to The Mountain Goats.

J. C. Otiono (she/they) is a Naijamerican poet and writer. She is working on a queer, dark speculative fiction manuscript about a haunted AI dating app. An absurdist, she believes being silly is a humble offering to the universe. She resides in what's essentially the wilderness of upstate New York. This was her first published work.

Rituja Patil is a queer poet from Mumbai, India. Their poetry has been published in *Violet, Indigo, Blue, Etc.*, *the licktey~split*, and *LiveWire*. They try to write poems that feel like a longing gaze at the ocean at night—sometimes it's quiet, sometimes stormy. They're also a law student on the side with research interests in intersections of personal liberty, bodily autonomy, and health care.

Isaac Pickell is a poet, PhD candidate, and adjunct instructor in Detroit. He is the author of *everything saved will be last* (Black Lawrence Press, 2021) and *It's not over once you figure it out* (Black Ocean, 2023), and his most recent work can be found at *Brevity*, *Copper Nickel*, and *Sundog Lit*. Isaac's taken a seat in all fifty states and has so much to look forward to.

Shannon Pulusan is a Fil-Am writer, illustrator, plant tita, and arts education administrator based in Jersey City. Her poetics explore how foodways, superstition, and the natural world can offer reparative insight and joy. Her poems appear in *Ecotone*, *Pigeon Pages*, *SRPR*, *underblong*, and more. She has received support from ARTS by the People, Bread Loaf Environmental Writers' Conference, and Brooklyn Poets, and she holds an MFA in Poetry from Rutgers University-Newark.

nat raum (they/them) is a queer disabled artist, writer, and editor based on unceded Piscataway and Susquehannock land in Baltimore. Past and upcoming homes for their work include *Split Lip Magazine*, *Baltimore Beat*, *Poet Lore*, *beestung*, and others.

Zoe Reay-Ellers is the proud EIC of the best dish soap-themed mag worldwide. She owns 20 plants and is currently an undergraduate student at Cornell. Her work has appeared in a number of places, including *Kissing Dynamite*, *HAD*, and *Fish Barrel Review*.

arushi (aera) rege is a queer, chronically-in-pain, Indian-American poet. A three-time Pushcart nominee, they are the proud author of *exit wound (no point* *of entry)*, BROWN GIRL EPIPHANY, and *suburban suicides*. They are the EIC of *ink&ivy lit* and *Bus Talk*.

heidi andrea restrepo rhodes is a queer, non-binary, crip/disabled, brown, writer, artist, scholar, educator, cultural worker, and creature of the Colombian diaspora. They are a poetry co-editor at *Apogee Journal* and their previously published works include: *The Inheritance of Haunting* (University of Notre Dame Press, 2019), *Ephemeral* (Ecotheo Collective, 2024), *Afterlives of Discovery: Speculative Geographies in the Settler Colonial Imaginary* (Duke University Press, 2025), and *Wayward Creatures* (Host Publications, 2025). They live in southern California.

Tristan Richards (she/her) is a poet from Minnesota, known for facilitating Unfold, a daily writing workshop each April. She has self-published two chapbooks: *Not All Challenges Are For Us* (2022) and *The Year Was Done Right* (2019); and has poems in *Talk Dirty to Me: The Anthology* and *Rabble Review*; *Gnashing Teeth*, ALOCASIA, *trampset*, and *Writers Resist*. Tristan is the recipient of a Professional Mid-Career Artist Grant from the Minnesota Prairie Lakes Regional Arts Council. She holds an MA from University of St. Thomas and a BA from Gustavus Adolphus College.

M.P. Rosalia is a writer and artist of many forms, enjoys exploring ideas about gods, identity, and time, and when not writing, likes to pet cats and climb trees.

Margaret Saigh is the author of three chapbooks and the creator of circlet, a poetry workshop and reading series. Her poems have been published widely in print and across the web. She received an MFA from the University of Pittsburgh.

Jake Salazar is a writer based in the Midwest, where he studies poetry at the University of Missouri, St. Louis. He is a member of the Lipan Apache Tribe of Texas. Jake currently lives in St. Louis with his two cats, both incisive critics.

Nnadi Samuel (he/him) holds a BA in English & Literature from the University of Benin. Author of *Nature Knows a Little About Slave Trade*, selected by Tate N. Oquendo (Sundress Publication, 2023). He is a 3x Best of the Net and 7x Pushcart nominee. He won the 2022 Angela C. Mankiewicz Poetry Contest,

River Heron Editor's Prize (2022), Bronze Prize for the Creative Future Writer's Award (2022), and recently won the Virginia Tech Center for Refugee, Migrants & Displacement Studies Annual Award (2023).

sangria (she/they) loves writing little in-jokes in her poetry for all to see. She has two cats and a hammock.

Mandy Seiner (she/they) is a writer, educator, and dill pickle connoisseur living in Brooklyn, New York. Her work has been published in *underblong*, *perhappened mag*, *Stone of Madness Press*, and elsewhere, and she is co-editor-in-chief of *DEAR Poetry Journal*. Talk to her about condiments, your favorite documentaries, and the use of pink peppercorn in unisex fragrances.

Ashish Kumar Singh (he/him) is a queer Indian poet with a Master's Degree in English Literature. His poems have appeared or are forthcoming in *Poetry Wales*, *The Stinging Fly*, *Frontier Poetry*, *The Bombay Literary Magazine*, *fourteen poems*, *The Texas Review*, *Atlanta Review*, *Foglifter*, *Diode*, and elsewhere. Currently, he is a PhD candidate at the University of Lucknow.

Derek R. Smith (he/him) is a public health professional, Anishinaabe two-spirit, uncle, sibling, partner, friend, who finds it hard to not write poetry. He has 2023 publications in *Great Lakes Review*, *¡Pa'lante!*, *euphony*, *Inlandia*, *Lucky Jefferson*, and others. There is no space for distance here, in poetry, and isn't that a beautiful thing?

Sarp Sozdinler has been published in *Electric Literature*, *The Kenyon Review*, *The Masters Review*, *trampset*, *JMWW*, and *The Normal School*, among other journals. Their work has been selected or nominated for anthologies including the Pushcart Prize, Best Small Fictions, and Wigleaf Top 50. They are currently working on their first novel in Philadelphia and Amsterdam.

Kit Steitz is a queer, non-binary poet from Columbia, Missouri or they could be a pothos named pathos, there's really no way to tell. They most enjoy writing poems while fending off slobbering, overgrown puppies and geriatric cats. Their work has appeared in *The Ivy Review*, *Moist Poetry Journal*, *the lickity~split*, and *JAKE*.

Liam Strong (they/them) is a queer neurodivergent cripple punk writer and photographer who owns two Squishmallows, three Buddhas, a VHS of *CATS The Musical*, and somewhere between four and eight jean jackets. They are the author of the chapbook *Everyone's Left the Hometown Show* (Bottlecap Press, 2023).

Joy Su is a poet and editor on the east coast who is urging you to support a free Palestine. You can find her work in *the lickety~split*, *the Augment Review*, and other assorted publications.

Saheed Sunday, NGP V, is a Nigerian poet, a Star Prize awardee, a 3x Pushcart Prize nominee, a Best of the Net nominee, Best Small Fictions nominee, an HCAF member, and a poetry reader at *Chestnut Review*. He won the Poetry Archive Now Contest, Centrestage Competition, Lagos Poem Project, Quramo Poetry Prize, ZODML Poetry Prize, and was a runner-up for The Nigeria Prize for Teen Authors. He was also shortlisted for the Rachel Wetzsteon Chapbook Award, Wingless Dreamer Poetry Prize, and The Breakbread Literacy Project. He has his works on *Palette Poetry*, *Lucent Dreaming*, *Lolwe*, *Strange Horizons*, *trampset*, *North Dakota Quarterly*, *The Deadlands*, *Shrapnel Magazine*, *Rough Cut Press*, *The Temz Review*, *Brittle Paper*, *Poetry Column*, *Off Topic Publishing*, *Eunoia Review*, and elsewhere. In 2018, he was shortlisted for the Wole Soyinka International Cultural Exchange Program.

Luke Sutherland is a trans writer and librarian. His work has appeared in *smoke and mold*, *ANMLY*, *Bright Wall/Dark Room*, *MQR: Mixtape*, and more. His chapbook, *Distance Sequence* (Neon Hemlock, 2024), won the OutWrite 2023 Chapbook Contest in Nonfiction. He was a finalist for the SmokeLong Quarterly Award for Flash Fiction in 2022, and the Larry Neal Writers' Award in 2023. Luke also helps run a DC-based trans writing group and micropress, Lilac Peril.

Dihya Tamaghza is a disabled Imazighen writer, artist, and scientist based in Scotland. When not writing, they can be found gardening, tending to their ever-growing animal family, and cooking up a storm. Their work has appeared in *Green Ink Poetry*, *The Ekphrastic Review*, *3rd Word Press*, among others.

Addie Tsai (any/all) is a queer nonbinary artist and writer of color. They collaborated with Dominic Walsh Dance Theater on *Victor Frankenstein* and *Camille Claudel*, among others. Addie has an MFA in Creative Writing from Warren Wilson College and a PhD in Dance from Texas Woman's University. She is the author of the queer Asian young adult novel *Dear Twin*. *Unwieldy Creatures*, their adult queer biracial retelling of *Frankenstein*, is from Jaded Ibis Press. They are the Fiction Co-Editor and Editor of Features & Reviews at *ANMLY*, Staff Writer at *Spectrum South*, and Founding Editor & Editor-in-Chief at *just femme & dandy*.

Ann Tweedy's first full-length book, *The Body's Alphabet* (Headmistress Press), earned a Bisexual Book Award and was a finalist for a Lambda Literary Award. Ann also has published three chapbooks: *Beleaguered Oases*, *White Out*, and *A Registry of Survival*. Her poems have appeared in *Rattle*, *Literary Mama*, *Naugatuck River Review*, and many other places, and she has been nominated for three Pushcart Prizes and five Best of the Net Awards. A law professor by day, Ann has devoted her career to serving Native Tribes. She recently moved to Mississippi from South Dakota.

Arya Vishin is a mixed Kashmiri-American & Jewish writer from San Jose, California. He is currently studying English & South Asian Studies @ UC Berkeley.

Nikki Wallschlaeger's work has been featured in *The Nation, Brick, American Poetry Review, Witness, The Kenyon Review, POETRY*, and others. She is the author of the full-length collections *Houses* (Horseless Press, 2015) and *Crawlspace* (Bloof, 2017), as well as the graphic book *I Hate Telling You How I Really Feel* (2019) from Bloof Books. She is also the author of an artist book called *Operation USA* through the Baltimore-based book arts group Container, a project acquired by Woodland Pattern Book Center in Milwaukee. Her third collection, *Waterbaby*, is out from Copper Canyon Press. She was a Visiting Associate Professor of Poetry at the Iowa Writer's Workshop from Spring 2021 to Spring 2022.

Sasha Weiss has a fainting problem, so they have to eat like 6 grams of salt a day to keep their blood pressure at normal levels. They've had chapbooks published by Blanket Sea Press and Bottlecap Press.

Keagan Wheat (he/they) is a trans, Latinx, disabled poet and artist from Houston. His work appears in *The Acentos Review, ANMLY, Variant Literature,* and more. His reviews of poetry and podcasts have been published in *Shards, Cutthroat,* and *Spectrum South.* He's a Pushcart Prize nominee and the winner of the 2024 Unity Committee Arts and Media Award. Keagan's read at Brooklyn Poets Staff Picks, Houston Public Poetry, the Poison Pen Reading Series, and the Houston Contemporary Arts Museum. His work has been supported by the New Orleans Poetry Festival, Lamplight AVL, and Letras Latinas.

Cassandra Whitaker (she/they) is a trans writer living in rural Virginia. Whit's work has been published in *Michigan Quarterly Review, beestung, Conjunctions, Lambda Literary Review, The Mississippi Review,* and other places. *Wolf Devouring A Wolf Devouring A Wolf* is out from Jackleg Press. They are a member of the National Book Critics Circle.

Elizabeth Wing is a writer and trailworker based in Portland, Oregon. Her short stories and poems have appeared in *Hanging Loose Magazine, The West Marin Review, 7×7, Up North Lit,* and numerous other venues. Wing wrote *Entanglement* under the mentorship of Joan Naviyuk Kane as part of her thesis work, *I WOULD NEVER THROW A FIRECRACKER INTO DRY GRASS, BUT*—at Reed College.

Anangookwe Wolf is a visual artist and poet currently based in Lenapehoking. They have performed at The Poetry Project, Kinstillatory Mappings in Light and Dark Matter, and you may find their poems in *Yellow Medicine Review.*

Julia Yong is a poet and perpetual student currently rooted in Philadelphia, PA. She is the Editor-in-Chief of Temple University's esteemed undergraduate literary and art magazine, *Hyphen.* Her poems have received recognition from The Academy of American Poets, SORTES, *JMWW,* and Moonstone Arts Center, among others.

Allya Yourish lives in Oregon with her wife and their small zoo. She was a nanny in France, a Fulbright grantee in Malaysia, a news assistant for *The New York Times,* and most recently, she received her MFA in Creative Writing and the

Environment from Iowa State University. Now, she works for a science museum and takes her breaks in the planetarium. Find her poems and nonfiction in the *North American Review*, ANMLY, *Hippocampus, Ecotone, Terrain*, and more.

Editors

Sarah Clark is a queer disabled two-spirit Nanticoke editor and cultural consultant. They are the editor-in-chief of *ALOCASIA*, a journal of queer planty writing. They are also the editor-in-chief and the poetry editor at *ANMLY*, editor-in-chief at *beestung*, a co-editor of the Bettering American Poetry series, and a board member at Sundress Publications. They have edited folios for publications including "GLITTERBRAIN" and "Indigenous Futures and Imagining the Decolonial" for *ANMLY*; "Sound Art," "Desire & Interaction," and a collection of global Indigenous art and literature, "First Peoples, Plural," for *Drunken Boat*; and "#NoDAPL #Still Here" for *Apogee Journal*; and their two series, "WE OUTLAST EMPIRE" and "Place[meant]," also at *Apogee Journal*. They have worked with a number of literary and arts publications and organizations, including *The Best of the Net, contemptorary, Glass: A Journal of Poetry, Blackbird, The Paris Review*, and elsewhere. Sarah's favorite plant is the *Cibotium barometz*. They live in Philadelphia with their partner.

Ashely Adams is a butch found in the Michigan woods. She has been published in *Permafrost, Flyway, The Fourth River*, and other places. More importantly, she has passed a Level 1 Venomous [Snake] Handling Course and is a certified storm spotter. Her favorite plant is *Pinus strobus*.